DEATH GLOBE!

'What's that?' Jenna enquired softly, lifting her head at a subdued yet persistent humming sound. It seemed to be coming from above their heads.

'I don't know,' Blake answered, perplexed, and then all three of them saw it, floating high up near the curved ceiling . . . a perfectly spherical globe which burned with a soft inner radiance. It was suspended in the air, drifting very slowly, and as they watched, fascinated, it began to pulse with a fierce radiant glow.

Jenna felt her senses start to slide. It wasn't unpleasant at first, this vague sliding world, until the voice began to hiss in her ear:

' . . . help me, Jenna, help me . . . they're hurting me, Jenna, help me . . . '

And then it wasn't pleasant at all, it was grotesque and frightening as images entered her mind and she was powerless to resist them . . .

BLAKE'S SEVEN

TERRY NATION'S
Blake's Seven

Novelisation by Trevor Hoyle

SPHERE BOOKS LIMITED
30/32 Gray's Inn Road, London WC1X 8JL

Published simultaneously in hardback by Arthur Barker Ltd
and paperback by Sphere Books Ltd 1977
Novelisation copyright © Trevor Hoyle 1977

Set in Intertype Times

Printed in Great Britain by
Hunt Barnard Printing Ltd,
Aylesbury, Bucks.

1

The concrete chamber was dank and bare. Caged wall lights glowed a dull red, making areas of shadowy darkness so that it seemed a place without dimensions, a lost corner of a labyrinthine basement stretching for miles beneath the city. Water dripped solemnly, like slow seconds, and there was the sour odour of dampness and decay.

Sub-Basement 43, Northern Perimeter, West-Europ Dome City.

It was a depressing hole and the last place Ravella would have chosen to be if she could have helped it. Waiting tensely in the shadows, she glanced upwards towards the stairway, the breath fluttering lightly in her nostrils. He should have been here by now. Pressing a button on her wrist chronometer, she read off the luminous digital display. Supposing something had gone wrong? Perhaps he had been apprehended and their plan discovered? But if she was going to panic over a slight delay she had no right to be –

A sound made her hold her breath. She stood quite still, listening, all her senses alert. Soft footsteps on the metal stairway. She strained to see in the gloom and made out the vague shape of a figure descending cautiously, testing the silence, watchful and uncertain.

The figure paused halfway. 'Ravella?'

She let go the air from her lungs and emerged from the

shadows: a slim, dark, attractive girl in her mid-twenties wearing the one-piece acrylic coverall of the Dome Dweller. The multi-coloured flash on her sleeve identified her as an electronics technician, grade three, in the Communications Division.

Everything was all right. It was Blake.

She called softly, 'I'm here,' and went swiftly to meet him at the foot of the stairs. 'Did you have any trouble?'

Blake looked nervously into the darkness. He shook his head. 'I followed the route you gave me. Didn't see anybody.' He wore the same type of one-piece coverall with the shoulder flash of the Engineering Division.

'Good.' Ravella became decisive. 'What about eating and drinking?' she asked him curtly. 'Have you managed to do without?'

'It's about thirty-six hours since I had anything.'

'And how do you feel?'

Blake grinned suddenly. 'Hungry and thirsty.'

'Nothing else?'

'I don't think so . . . ' He didn't seem entirely certain. 'Though I'm not sure, I can't describe it . . . '

'More alert? More – receptive?'

She watched him, knowing the confused thoughts that must be in his head. They had certainly got to him, Ravella thought. She didn't know his age but guessed he was in his early thirties, an imposing figure with a broad, solid torso and an unmistakably powerful set to his shoulders. His hair was thick and wiry, and dark – the same dark brown as his eyes, which were now shadowed with uncertainty, but which – she knew – could flash with a searing fire.

Blake shook his head uncertainly. 'Tense is a better word. Most likely the excitement of breaking the rules by coming here –'

'It's not that,' Ravella said peremptorily. 'All our food and drink is treated with suppressants. Going without anything to eat or drink for a day and a half, the effect is beginning to wear off.'

'Oh come on,' Blake protested. 'You don't believe all those stories about our food being drugged, do you? It's one of those myths that's been going round for centuries.'

'It happens to be true,' Ravella asserted quietly.

Blake raised his eyebrows, smiling gently. 'Nonsense. If you believe –'

Ravella grasped his arm and pulled him into the shadows. There was somebody on the stairway. They waited, breathing tensely, and then Ravella relaxed her grip when she saw it was Dal. The young man came quickly down into the chamber, his keen blue eyes searching the darkness, and Ravella ran to him and they embraced. Blake stood to one side, not wishing to intrude, feeling slightly uncomfortable. He was beginning to have doubts about being here at all; there was something he couldn't quite grasp, a vague unease that he couldn't define . . .

Ravella beckoned him forward and introduced them.

'Dal Richie. Roj Blake. Dal is with the Hydroponic Division, Level 19.'

The two men shook hands.

'I've been looking forward to meeting you,' said Dal Richie, an edge of excitement to his voice. He looked at Blake intently, his manner one of guarded respect, as if meeting somebody whose reputation had preceded him. 'I hear you have a family on one of the outer systems.'

'That's right,' Blake affirmed. 'My parents and a brother and sister. They're on Ziegler 5.'

'It's a nice planet, so I'm told.' Dal Richie's eyes seemed to harden momentarily. 'A bit like Earth used to be.'

'They seem to like it.'

'You hear from them much?'

'I get tape letters a couple of times a year. Ravella told me you might have some news of them.'

Dal Richie shook his head. 'No, not me. The man we're

going to meet—' He glanced at Ravella, and then went on, 'He was on Ziegler 5 a few months ago. He specially asked us to contact you so he could pass the message along in person.'

'How do I get to meet him? Where is he?'

'He's waiting for us,' Ravella said smoothly. 'Outside.'

Blake was shocked. He stared at her. 'Outside . . . ?'

'Don't look so worried,' Dal Richie reassured him briskly. 'It's not all that bad. The air is fresh, so it smells different. It might be a bit colder, and if you're lucky you could even feel rain.' His youthful face lit up in a grin. 'Ever been in rain?'

'We'd better get started,' Ravella interjected, consulting her digital chronometer.

'Outside?' Blake said worriedly. He hadn't bargained on this.

'Through there,' Dal Richie said crisply, pointing to a heavy metal door set deeply into the concrete wall.

So that was the way Outside. Blake shuddered involuntarily. All of his thirty-five years had been spent inside the Dome; nobody ever ventured Outside, at least not of their own free will. Was it really worth it to have news of his family? He couldn't remember the last time he had been afraid.

He started as Dal Richie touched his arm. 'It's only fair to warn you,' the young man said, his face serious. 'Going outside the Dome is a Category Six crime. If you're caught there'll be punishments and special treatments. It'll go on your record – and that'll mean however good you are in your job you'll never get promoted to a senior echelon. You understand?'

Blake gazed at the door while he decided. He looked at the young man, saw something in his eyes that seemed to give him confidence. He nodded slowly.

'One more thing,' Ravella cautioned him in a low voice. 'Whoever you see, whatever you hear tonight, you keep silent about. If you report anything to the authorities you'll find yourself more deeply implicated than you can imagine.'

Blake looked from one to the other. 'I understand.'

Dal Richie led the way across the chamber, taking a small black instrument from his pocket. Blake watched fascinated as the young man activated the device, which emitted a low pulsing hum, and scanned the lock.

'Vibra lock-pick,' Dal Richie explained as he worked. 'Give me two minutes and it should be *Open Sesame* . . . '

Ravella had moved silently to the stairway. She peered upwards, frowning.

'What is it?' Blake asked in a whisper. 'Did you hear something?'

'I thought so.' She turned away, shaking her head, and came back. 'Nothing. Must have been my imagination.'

Dal Richie had completed his lock-picking activities. Now he took out a metre length of cable with a spring-loaded clamp at either end, fastened one clamp to the metal door-frame and the other to the door itself. 'If you open the door it breaks a circuit and a fault is registered on the security computer.' He flashed a brief mischievous smile at Blake. 'This keeps the circuit intact.' He straightened up. 'Ready?'

Ravella nodded, her slim body tensed and waiting. Blake was about to say something and then changed his mind. He had come this far, he would go through with it: if the girl was prepared to venture Outside, so was he.

Dal Richie slowly turned the handle and the heavy metal door opened. Cold night air swirled in and Blake took a deep steadying breath. So this was what fresh air tasted like . . . not as bad as he had feared. Ravella stepped through the doorway and he followed her, Dal Richie close behind, shutting the door after them.

Blake couldn't believe it: for the first time in his life he had left the protective sanctuary of the Dome. He was Outside!

As the door closed behind them the hidden watcher at the

top of the stairway slid from the shadows and began silently to descend.

They had been travelling for thirty minutes or so, Blake estimated, though he had no idea of the distance they might have covered. The terrain was a mixture of thick undergrowth and rocky outcrops, and in the almost pitch blackness he had to rely on his companions' sense of direction; alone he would have been totally lost.

Dal Richie had halted and was crouched by a jumble of rock. He gestured Blake and Ravella to come forward and said in a low voice:

'I'll check ahead. Watch for my signal.'

When he had gone, swallowed up in the encroaching darkness, Ravella surprised Blake by cupping her hands to drink from a small stream which trickled through the rocks. She saw his expression and invited him to try some. He hesitated – then in a hurried movement scooped up a handful and drank it. It almost seemed to sting his mouth, it was so cold and sharp, and he pulled a wry face.

'Natural water,' Ravella informed him. Her face was a pale oval in the gloom, and he could see that she was grinning. 'The stuff we get in the Dome has been recycled a thousand times. It's been filtered, treated and dosed with suppressant.'

'I like it better than this,' Blake told her sourly.

Ravella knelt up and faced him abruptly; she seemed almost angry about something. 'Doesn't it bother you that you spend your life in a state of drug-induced tranquility?' she demanded. 'Do you like the idea that you've been turned into some sort of robot?'

'You don't know what you're talking about,' Blake said dismissively. 'It makes no sense. Just tell me why . . . why should the Administration want to doctor our food with drugs?'

12

Ravella clenched her fists. 'Because it's the only way they can keep control over eight hundred million people. There – in that city,' and she pointed to where the light from the Dome was reflected in the night sky. 'And do you want to know why they've been stepping up the suppressants?'

Blake watched her, his face clouded with uncertainty.

'Because the number of dissidents is growing. People like Dal and me. We've seen what's happening and we want to stop it before it goes too far.'

'Stop *what*?' Blake asked her, bewildered by her fervour. 'What more do you want? We're fed, clothed, sheltered. They look after us if we're sick. Our intellectual and emotional needs are satisfied on the Sublim-circuits.' He shook his head perplexedly. 'What more could we need?'

Ravella gazed at him. 'Don't you know?' she said softly.

Blake stared blankly into the darkness. 'I know I'm content.'

'They really cleaned your head out, didn't they?'

'What do you mean?' Blake asked sharply, snapping back to look at her.

'Don't you remember *anything* about the treatments they gave you?'

'I've had no treatments,' Blake maintained stolidly.

'It's hard to believe. I thought there'd be something left ... some trace of memory.' She looked sorrowful, downcast.

Blake sighed impatiently. 'Look, I'm sorry, I just don't know what you're getting at. What is it about my memory? And what are these treatments – ?'

Ravella held up her hand. Not far away a lamp had blinked: the signal they were waiting for. 'It's all clear. We can go in.'

She went quickly across the small clearing keeping low to the ground; Blake followed, stumbling in the darkness and cursing under his breath. What was she getting at, he wondered. There was something odd about all this; a persistent nagging unease hovered on the edge of his mind, taunting

13

him like an unsolved riddle. It didn't make sense, any of it, and yet . . .

But there wasn't time to think. He tried to keep up with her. She was younger and fitter, darting through the undergrowth like a young gazelle. Blake was confused now, not knowing what to expect – but whatever he might have imagined lay ahead he was completely unprepared for the sight that was to confront him.

Pausing by a sheer rock face, Ravella deftly took his hand in hers and led him into a cavern lit by flickering torches. In the murky light he saw, conversing quietly in small groups of two or three, about twenty people who immediately fell silent the moment they entered. Blake took in several confused impressions all at once: the strange costumes of some of the people, which appeared to be a weird mixture of synthetic materials and animal skins, patched with leather and held together by thongs. The people themselves were rough-looking and unkempt, with matted hair and long beards, and he was aware of their curious, almost suspicious scrutiny. It was like suddenly coming upon a scene from the Stone Age.

There were Dome Dwellers here too, he realised after a moment, wearing the standard-issue acrylic coverall with its identifying shoulder flash. While he was still taking it all in, trying to comprehend it, a tall man with a lean intelligent face and white hair, who had been talking with Dal Richie, came across and greeted him warmly. He was about forty, Blake surmised, wearing a style of clothing he couldn't recall ever having seen before.

'Roj – good to see you! It's been a long time.'

Blake was taken aback. As they shook hands he said hesitantly, 'Nice to see you, but I . . . '

'I'm sorry,' the man said immediately, his expression pained. 'That was stupid of me. Of course you won't remember. Bran Foster. I would have been one of the people they blanked off.'

14

'Blanked off?' Blake said, frowning with sudden irritation. 'Look, will somebody tell me what this is all about? Ravella keeps dropping hints about my memory and about treatments – I've had no treatments and my memory is fine. Now just what is all this?'

'I know, I know,' Bran Foster said placatingly. 'I realise it's difficult for you. And it's just as difficult for all of us who knew you before. The important thing is that you're here. It gives us a chance to explain and try and make you understand.'

'I wish you would,' Blake said grimly.

Bran Foster's attention was caught by three new arrivals. He touched Blake's arm and said, 'Excuse me for a moment. Tarrant has just arrived and I must have a word with him. I'll be right back.'

He turned away and Blake saw him shake hands with a rather serious-looking man with blond hair who was standing alone near the cavern entrance.

Who were all these people, Blake wondered. What was the purpose of this meeting, held in secret outside the Dome City? He had come here for no other reason than to receive word of his family, so just what was going on? He felt on edge and the suspicion lurked at the back of his mind that he had been tricked into coming here . . . but for what purpose? What did they want with him?

Turning to Dal Richie, he said, 'These primitive-looking people in animal skins – they're Outsiders, aren't they?'

Dal Richie nodded, his keen blue eyes surveying the murmuring groups in the smoky flickering light of the torches. 'Yes, there are quite a few of them working for our cause now.'

'But once a person is condemned to live outside the city it's treasonable to have any contact with him.'

'That's right,' said Dal Richie calmly. He seemed unperturbed. 'But then, this whole meeting is treasonable. If it wasn't so important we wouldn't be taking the risk.'

'I'm getting out of here,' Blake informed him brusquely. 'I want nothing to do with it. You simply told me I was going to meet a man who had some news about my family – that was all and nothing more. I'm not going to get mixed up in all this.' He started to move towards the cavern entrance. 'I'm going back.'

Dal Richie grabbed his arm. 'Hold on a minute. You ought to hear what Foster has to say first.'

Blake shook him off. 'I don't want to hear,' he told the young man with a flare of irritation. 'I should do my duty and report everything I've seen to the Administration.'

Ravella observed him coolly. 'You can't do that,' she said in a quiet even tone.

'Just how do you propose to stop me?' Blake asked, meeting her look squarely.

'We've taken precautions,' said Dal Richie, his voice bland and expressionless. 'There are certain documents in the city. They happen to have your signature on them – forged, of course. But convincing enough to implicate you in everything we've been doing over the past few months. Don't have any doubts: one word in the wrong place can make you look as guilty as any of us.'

So it was a set-up. They'd planned it all down to the last detail. Blake felt a wave of anger rise up inside him and he lost control – grabbing wildly at the young man, feeling the need to lash out in blind frustration. Ravella hung on to Blake's arm, struggling to restrain him.

'All right, that's enough!' Bran Foster's imperative command rang out and he pulled Blake away. 'Leave us alone for a minute,' he instructed Dal Richie and the girl. Then, taking Blake to one side, he spoke in a low, urgent voice:

'Now calm down. First of all listen to what I have to tell you. After that you can do whatever you want.'

Blake regarded the tall white-haired man resentfully. He took a deep steadying breath and said, 'All right, now what is it you know about my family?'

'I'll come to that. There are some other things you should know first.'

'Forget the other things!' Blake erupted. 'Just tell me what you know!'

Bran Foster's eyes went hard and cold. His jaw tightened and he said brutally, 'They're dead. Your parents. Your brother. Your sister. All four of them are dead!'

Blake stared at him in stunned silence. The man was lying. It was another trick; more cunning deceit. He refused to believe it.

'I'm sorry,' Bran Foster said, his voice softening. 'I didn't intend you should hear it like that.' He seemed genuinely contrite. 'They were executed four years ago. Just after your trial.'

'*Four years ago?*' Blake said incredulously. 'No, it isn't true.' He shook his head stubbornly. 'I still hear from them. I had a voice tape just a few months ago. They're fine – they can't be dead!'

'Listen to me,' Bran Foster said urgently. 'The voice tapes are all forgeries. Do you understand? They're part of the treatment to keep your memory suppressed.' He sighed and laid his hand on Blake's shoulder. 'Look, this is going to be hard for you . . . but I have to tell you things about yourself of which you have no memory. Now just hear me out.'

Blake felt as if his mind was spinning in a vacuum. None of this made any sense. He pressed his fingers to his temples in order to steady his confused thoughts. 'Go on,' he said between his teeth.

Bran Foster glanced round, aware of the attention that was focused on them by the other groups. This was going to be difficult enough without an audience, he realised, and gestured towards a quieter part of the cavern, just inside the entrance. The two men found a place to sit among a small pile of rocks, facing one another.

Bran Foster studied his hands for a moment while he considered how best to begin. Then he took a breath. 'I've got to go back just over four years. There was a good deal of discontent with the Administration. There were several activist groups but the only one that really meant anything was led by a man called . . . Roj Blake.'

He smiled faintly as Blake's eyes came up to meet his. Their expression was blank, uncomprehending.

'Yes, you,' Bran Foster went on, with more emphasis. 'There were a lot of people who believed in you. You and I worked together very closely. We were outlawed and hunted but we had friends and supporters and we were really beginning to get somewhere. Then we were betrayed,' he said, his voice suddenly adopting a harsher tone. 'I still don't know who gave us away . . . but in the end you were captured. So were most of our followers.'

Blake had begun to experience instantaneous subliminal impressions, as if emanating from a locked corner of his mind. They were like the distorted fragments of a three-dimensional holograph flickering in a limbo of dead time – long ago and far away on the far side of an impenetrable barrier.

'The Administration could have disposed of you, had you killed,' Bran Foster's voice went on steadily, 'but that would have given the cause a martyr.'

As if in a nightmarish vision he saw hands reaching for him, huge white hairless hands, and then he was thrown violently to the ground, surrounded by grey-uniformed security guards who beat at him with black bully-sticks, their leering faces coming nearer and then receding as if in some grotesque ritual dance. The vision was frighteningly real . . .

'Instead they put you into intensive treatment,' Bran Foster's voice intoned. 'They erased specialist areas of your memory and implanted new ideas. They all but took you to pieces and rebuilt you. And when you were ready you broadcast a public statement.'

Now the image had changed and he was strapped to a

18

bench. They were doing something to his head. He couldn't see what it was but he felt the cold malignant sensation of metal against his forehead and temples . . . and then the vision shimmered under the onslaught of blinding white pain that seemed to sear through every cell of his brain. He felt his mind slipping away into greyness and it was as if he were falling away from himself, his own anguished face slowly vanishing in a gathering cloud of grey mist . . .

'You said that you'd been misguided. You appealed to everybody to support the Administration and to hound out the traitors. You were very good,' Bran Foster said, his voice barely above a whisper. 'Very convincing.'

Blake shuddered and stared down at his clenched fists. His face was bathed in sweat. He moistened his lips and said quietly, 'And the others . . . what happened to them?'

'To make themselves look benevolent the Administration allowed them to emigrate to the outer systems. Like your family,' Bran Foster told the ashen man in front of him, 'they were executed on arrival.'

Blake struggled to take it all in. There was still much he did not understand; it was as if portions of his memory had been walled off with lead shielding, like the core in a nuclear reactor, and he had only the vaguest notion of what was hidden there, locked away from his conscious perceptions.

He looked up to meet Bran Foster's forthright gaze. 'Why are you telling me this now?' he asked dully.

Bran Foster leaned forward, his lean intelligent face coming alive. 'Because we're getting ready to move again. To take action against the Administration. If it was known that you were here with us we'd get tremendous support.'

'I see.'

'Will you, Roj?' He hung on Blake's answer. 'Will you work with us?'

'I don't know . . . ' Blake shook his head uncertainly. 'It's all too fast for me. I'm not even sure I believe everything you've told me.'

'It's true, every word of it.'

'I'd like to think about these things for a while. Do you mind?'

Bran Foster stood up. 'Take all the time you want. I'll get this meeting started. We'll talk again when we've finished.' He smiled reassuringly and returned to the main area of the cavern.

Dal Richie, Ravella and Tarrant had been discussing what long-term effects the process of mental manipulation might have had on Blake. They paused as Bran Foster joined them and all four turned to observe Blake, who had risen and was standing, disconsolate and alone, at the entrance to the cavern.

Dal Richie looked questioningly at Bran Foster, whose expression was sober and withdrawn.

'What do you think?' the young man asked, voicing the question uppermost in all their minds.

'I don't know.' Bran Foster gnawed his lower lip. 'There's nothing much left of the man I knew. We'll just have to wait and see.'

They watched as Blake wandered aimlessly from the cavern, obviously plagued by doubt. It would take time – a great deal of time, Bran Foster told himself – for his old friend to pick up the pieces of his shattered past. Perhaps he would never make it. The Administration were exceedingly thorough in their methods. Especially when it was someone like Blake, who had been such a powerful and disruptive influence.

And yet he was vital to the cause – with Blake on their side they could at last begin to make real progress in their fight against the evil and corrupt forces which held sway over all their lives.

He mentally shook himself, casting aside these somewhat morose reflections, and stepped into the centre of the cavern, his voice ringing out authoritatively.

'If you'll all gather round we'll get this meeting started.

There are a number of important matters to be discussed.'

The Dome Dwellers and Outsiders fell silent and drew near in hushed expectancy.

Blake sat slumped on a rock, gazing upwards with dull eyes at the night sky. He had never known that the stars were so bright. Having lived his entire life within the confines of the Dome he had been used to seeing them as an indistinct glimmer of light, a diffuse blur beyond the curving thermoplastic shell. But they were really incredibly vivid: a magnificent glittering panorama spread across the heavens.

It was no good. Blake wrenched his mind back to grim, inescapable reality. Sooner or later he would have to confront the enigma of his lost past. The starscape was but a temporary distraction that his mind had fastened on in the forlorn hope of pushing aside the tortured questions that were hammering in his brain. Had Foster spoken the truth? Was it actually true that the Administration had done something to his mind, erasing whole segments of memory? In one way he couldn't believe it; a persistent inner voice told him that it was nonsense; and yet while Bran Foster had talked he had received from somewhere deep in his subconscious fleeting images of terrifying events that seemed to have happened long ago – not to him, but to someone else ... a stranger.

Another Roj Blake.

A faint sound on the breeze made him instantly alert. Somebody or something was moving through the undergrowth. Rising quickly to his feet, Blake strained to see in the enclosing darkness.

There it was again – a rustling of branches as if someone was creeping stealthily nearer. Swiftly, and not a moment too soon, he stepped behind a jumbled pile of rock and crouched down, and in that same instant distinctly saw two shadowy figures crossing the small clearing. They came to within three metres of his hiding-place, close enough for him to see that they carried weapons of some kind.

Blake felt his throat constrict. The distinctive snub-nosed shape of the V-911 para-handgun issued only to the guards of the Security Division. He pressed himself against the rock, hardly daring to breathe.

There was a subdued bleeping sound and one of the guards unhooked a two-way communicator from his belt and thumbed a button.

'Report.'

'All units in position,' came the terse reply.

'Understood. Out.'

The guard returned the communicator to his belt and nodded slowly to his companion, as if in confirmation that everything was going according to plan.

Slowly, and with the utmost caution, Blake attempted to move deeper into the covering undergrowth. In an obscure way that he didn't understand it seemed imperative that he warn Bran Foster and the others: on the evidence before him, this seemed like a full-scale operation – and the Security Division wasn't noted for its gentle, considerate handling of Dome Dwellers who broke all the rules and regulations by going Outside.

The two guards remained motionless, looking away into the darkness, their attitude suggesting that they were awaiting a signal.

Using the rock as cover, Blake edged backwards. He started to turn, crouched on all-fours, and there was an almost imperceptible sound as a dead twig snapped beneath his foot.

Blake froze, the breath locked tight in his chest.

One of the guards looked round, raising the blunt snout of his para-handgun, and advanced towards the rock. He had only to look beyond it to see Blake, exposed and helpless, without a prayer of reaching the dense covering of greenery. Discovery seemed inevitable; the guard's head loomed above him, a sheen of light reflected on the curved visor of his helmet, and his companion broke the pressing silence.

'There it is!'

A green light winking from across the clearing.

The guard turned away and quickly unhooked the communicator from his belt. He pressed the transmit button and uttered a brief command, a harder edge to his voice.

'All units move in!'

They moved swiftly and silently away, gliding like ominous shadows in the direction of the cavern. Blake emerged from behind the rock. It was too late, he could do nothing. Better to return to the city while he had the chance. He started to cross the clearing but had gone no more than a few paces when something stopped him. He couldn't leave them: every instinct was urging him to do what he could to help, even at the risk of his own safety and well-being.

Bran Foster had awakened certain disturbing events in his memory, just for a short while had penetrated the grey blanket of the past, and, if for no other reason, Blake owed him something for that.

The white-haired man had an air of quiet authority. He spoke in an even, unhurried tone to the small gathering that was but one tiny fragment of a movement that was growing stronger day by day.

The group listened intently, the torchlight making shifting patterns on their serious, determined faces.

'Settlers in many of the outer systems are demanding greater autonomy. If their voices can be unified, the Administration will have to listen. The security forces are already stretched. If our campaign of civil disobedience here on Earth is stepped up, they'll have to concentrate their forces here, and that will give the outer systems much more freedom of action.' Bran Foster held up his right fist and clasped it firmly in his left palm. 'Our aim is to have at least one world declare its independence within the next two years.'

At this there was a low murmur of approval from Dome Dwellers and Outsiders alike; in this they shared a common goal.

Dal Richie stood up and the gathering quietened.

'In the next few months we want to cause as much disruption as possible in the food manufacturing divisions. There is nothing more effective than ration cuts to cause unrest.' He pulled a sheaf of papers from a vinyl pouch. 'I've listed the methods by which this disruption can be implemented.'

He handed the sheets to Ravella, who helped distribute them. She could tell from their expressions that many of the people were glad that at last there was to be positive action against the Administration. This was why they had risked their lives by coming here. And if Blake would only agree to join their cause, it wouldn't be long before their efforts began to have real effect.

A curved polished surface caught her eye and she looked up, puzzled and distracted, and the blood seemed to solidify in her veins.

A line of black-helmeted security guards blocked the entrance, their para-handguns pointed unwaveringly at the assembly. It had been a very silent invasion, so much so that it was several moments before the murmur of voices fell away to an absolute stunned silence.

Before anyone could react, or do anything foolish, Bran Foster stepped quickly forward, holding out his arms in a gesture that was at once calming and conciliatory.

'There will be no attempt to resist arrest,' he told his silent followers. 'No matter what the provocation there will be no resort to violence.'

He faced the leader of the force, a short bulky man with the insignia of a captain on his sleeve.

'We claim our rights as citizens and demand that we be treated as civil prisoners.'

The captain stared at him, betraying no emotion. Then, with the most indifferent and economical of movements, he pressed the button and fired a blast at point-blank range. There was an intense burst of searing flame, a crackle of discharged energy, and Bran Foster was enveloped in a brilliant glowing halo of red.

Instantly he fell to the ground, the force-field dispersing round his lifeless body.

The guards moved forward in a solid line, their weapons raised and ready for firing.

Outside, Blake heard a fierce and prolonged crackling roar and saw the cavern entrance light up. He stood, transfixed with horror, as the mingled sounds of screams came to his ears, hardly believing what was taking place. Then, as the full terrible reality of it came to him he slumped to his knees and buried his head in his hands. After a while there was no other sound on the night air except for the muffled sobs he could no longer contain.

The dawn light revealed the full extent of the massacre. The security force had done its job with great expediency. Blake ventured slowly into the cavern, seeing the huddled bodies in a kind of dazed dream. He approached the corpse of Bran Foster, lying crookedly on its side, and touched the face of the dead man.

An emotion rose up inside him, a cold and deadly sense of purpose that seemed to burn steadily like a hard flame; with an almost savage movement he stood up and looked for one last time at the dreadful scene, then turned abruptly on his heel and left the cavern.

He now knew, without the slightest doubt, what had to be done. He was filled with a fierce resolve that quickened his pace as he returned to the Dome City.

Arriving at the outer door he was relieved to find it still unlocked. It was fortunate that the security forces hadn't checked the basement during the night. Slipping cautiously inside, he moved swiftly across the darkened area to the stairway, and was about to ascend when everything was flooded with harsh, brilliant light.

His hand gripping the rail, Blake looked at the row of guards lining the walls of the chamber. Slowly he raised his head and gazed up at the squat figure of the captain, standing above him, a para-handgun clamped in his hairy fist. This time there was no escape.

2

'Can he break through the memory blocks, Dr Havant?'

Ven Glynd, his eyes fixed on the scanner-screen, spoke over his shoulder to the man seated on the other side of the desk. The screen showed a tiny windowless cell, with blank white walls, a chair, a bed, and little else to relieve its drab anonymity. The man seated on the chair was hunched forward, his fingers pressed over his eyes as if in an anguish of remembering.

'Possible but unlikely,' said Dr Havant stiffly. He was a rather stern-looking man in his forties, not much given to smiling. 'We don't eradicate memory, we simply make it inaccessible. In a normal, healthy mind the barriers are impenetrable. But should he suffer anything like a nervous breakdown, where all the mental circuitry malfunctions, then he might, as it were, find a route into his past.'

Glynd turned away from the screen; he was sleek and well-groomed and even his immaculately-tailored coverall couldn't disguise his corpulent frame. The flash on his shoulder identified him as a high-ranking member of the Justice Department. He nodded slowly, his eyes narrowed and scheming. 'I see. That might prove a problem.'

'Can he not simply be eliminated?' Havant enquired.

'No.' This spoken quietly but with emphasis by Alta Morag, a young, attractive, yet rather cold woman who sat

27

alongside Dr Havant. 'For many people he still symbolises opposition to the Administration.'

'Is that true?'

Ven Glynd nodded. 'We've done psych readings on cross-sections of the community. They show a fairly high per-centage of people, particularly the younger ones, who believe that Blake's trial was a show-piece and that his statements were rigged.' He shrugged slightly. 'Which of course is true.'

'His death could be used by the dissidents,' Alta Morag added. 'They need a hero and, alive or dead, Blake could be it.'

'Difficult . . . ' Dr Havant mused, examining his manicured fingernails. He went on in a thoughtful tone, 'I suppose my department could induce a disease . . . something rapidly progressive. Terminal. Would his natural death help?'

'I don't think so,' Ven Glynd said doubtfully. 'It could still arouse sympathy.'

Alta Morag agreed. 'Ideally what we need is something to discredit him that will result in a deportation order. If he could be committed to Cygnus Alpha . . . '

She pursed her lips together, pondering this, and then a slow cunning smile began to form on her beautiful face. She said softly, 'I think I'm on to something. Doctor, am I right in thinking that you can not only eliminate memory, but that you can also create experiences and implant them into subjects so that they will believe they really happened?'

'Of course. In fact, creating an illusion of reality is quite simple.'

'Good.' Alta Morag looked triumphantly at Glynd. 'Then I think we can totally destroy his credibility and get him sentenced.' She rose at once and went towards the main door of the office. 'Would you come with me, Doctor? I'll explain what I have in mind.'

Havant followed her. 'Of course.'

Alta Morag paused at the door. 'I'll report back as soon as

we've done a feasibility check,' she told the large sleek man behind the desk.

'All right. As quick as you can. We have to bring charges within the next twenty-four hours.'

Ven Glynd waited until the door had closed and then crossed to an inner door, opening it to admit someone who had been waiting in the next room.

'They've gone.' Glynd moved to the desk. 'Did you hear all that?'

The man came slowly and purposefully into the room, his soft cloth shoes making no sound on the deep pile of the carpet. He sat down and made himself comfortable. 'Yes, I heard.'

'Satisfied?'

'No.' This in a deceptively soft tone that concealed an underlying strain of vehement feeling. 'He can identify me. My whole operation is at risk while he's alive. I'll be satisfied only when that risk is eliminated.'

Ven Glynd glanced at the screen. The man in the cell was in the same position, still attempting to fill the gaps in his shattered memory.

A key turned in the lock and the door opened to reveal a fresh-faced young man who entered cheerfully, carrying a briefcase. 'I'll call you when I'm ready to leave,' he told the warder, and held out his hand to Blake, who was regarding him blankly, wondering who the devil he could be.

'How do you do? I'm Tel Varon,' the young man informed him briskly. He pointed to his shoulder flash. 'Justice Department. I've been assigned to defend you.'

'I won't need a defence. I'm going to plead guilty.'

Tel Varon looked pained. 'Come now, I'm sure we don't need to go that far. Certainly the evidence against you is –' he coughed ' – strong, but –'

'I just want the opportunity to make a statement in open

court. I want to be certain that those responsible for the massacre are brought to trial.'

The young man regarded him in a puzzled fashion. 'I'm sorry . . . ?'

'It was murder,' Blake said grimly. 'I grant that the meeting was an illegal assembly, and that the people involved were members of an Anti-Administration group. But there can be no justification for their slaughter.'

Tel Varon had listened to this with growing bewilderment.

'Look, er, I'm afraid we're at cross purposes somewhere. There's nothing in the charges against you about illegal assembly.' He shook his head emphatically. 'No, no, nothing like that. You're not being prosecuted under the political code . . . it's a straightforward criminal action.'

Blake frowned. 'Criminal?' He said curiously, 'Look, just what are the charges?'

Tel Varon delved into his briefcase. 'I have them right here,' he said, producing a sheet of paper. He scanned it briefly. 'There are a number of counts. Assault on a minor. Lewd and indecent behaviour. Attempting to corrupt minors and –'

Blake snatched the paper from him. 'Let me see that.' He read it disbelievingly, with growing agitation. 'This is disgusting – all involving children. None of this is true!'

The young man nodded knowingly, yet his eyes sought to look away. 'Of course not,' he murmured, 'of course not. That's why you alarmed me when you said you'd plead guilty – '

'Not to this!' Blake protested. 'Not to these charges!'

'They're the only ones that have been brought against you. And, I must tell you frankly – ' he coughed nervously once again ' – well, the evidence against you is, er, very damaging.'

'If there is any evidence, then it's been faked,' Blake told him hotly.

'Well . . . I think that might be quite hard to prove. I've

had the opportunity of talking to the children – that is, the prosecution witnesses – and they, well they do seem very certain of their facts.'

Blake nodded slowly. He was beginning to see. It was a set-up.

'Yes,' he said. 'Yes, I'm sure that briefing will have been perfect...'

'If I may, I'd like to outline how I think we should conduct our case –'

Blake cut him short. 'What's the point? They've set me up beautifully.'

'There is a possible approach,' Tel Varon said, determined to do his job properly. 'If we could cite your record ... your breakdown after your involvement with those, er, illegal political groups; what was it – four years ago now? The remorse that you felt. The guilt you carried has placed you under an enormous strain. We can submit that these assaults ... these aberrations ... were carried out whilst you were mentally unbalanced.'

Blake turned on him. His expression was contorted with anger but his voice was deadly calm. 'I'll plead guilty and offer no defence.'

Tel Varon held up his hand. 'That might prove foolhardy. These are grave charges and without extenuating circumstances you might face deportation. A mental institution would be better than spending the rest of your life on Cygnus Alpha.'

'You will plead guilty and offer no defence.' Blake's face was a grim, determined mask. 'Is that understood?'

Tel Varon heaved a sigh and nodded reluctantly. He tucked his briefcase under his arm and rapped on the door. He thought for a moment and then offered his final piece of advice. 'You're taking a very serious course. Won't you reconsider?'

Blake shook his head stubbornly. 'The Administration is out to get me. And as far as I can see, they've won. If I plead diminished responsibility, then I'm branded as mentally unstable. Even if you could prove me totally innocent, the charges have been made. The mud will stick. For a lot of people I'll always be a child molester.' A sour smile twisted his features. 'I've got to hand it to them: they've done a brilliant job.'

The cell door opened, and Tel Varon, after a moment's hesitation, shrugged and quickly went out.

Blake began to pace the cramped cell, hemmed in by the walls, the bed, the single upright chair. He knew that every minute of the day and night he was being observed by the camera mounted high in one corner, its glinting wide-angle lens covering every square centimetre of the tiny space. A spasm of fury shook him, and in a sudden release of helpless frustration he picked up the chair and swung it at the impersonal, all-seeing eye.

The courtroom was austere, almost classical in its simplicity. Like all the rooms in the Dome City, it had no windows to mar its bland uniformity. The dominant feature was a computer console against one wall, standing silent and inactive as the officials of the court busied themselves in preparation for the trial.

Wearing the ribbon of the legal representative of the accused, Tel Varon sorted through his papers, occasionally glancing towards Alta Morag, who wore the ribbon of the prosecution team; she stood quietly conversing with Ven Glynd, the pair of them exuding an air of smug confidence.

There was a slight stirring of interest among the observers seated at the rear of the courtroom as Blake, accompanied by a guard, appeared at a side door and was brought forward to join his advocate.

'Good morning,' Tel Varon greeted him. He noted a change of mood in his client, which was confirmed when Blake said:

'I've had a chance to think things through. It's vital that I have an opportunity to make a statement to the court.'

Tel Varon appraised him doubtfully. 'That's up to the Arbiter. It's not usual,' he added cautiously.

'You must try. Look, there's no way I can prove my innocence, is there?'

'You've given me no chance to try,' Tel Varon reproached him.

'If I had, could you have changed things?' Blake demanded with a touch of sarcasm.

Tel Varon agreed that it was doubtful under the circumstances.

'You know as well as I do,' Blake went on, 'that we're just going through formalities. But I swear to you that I'm innocent. The charges are totally fabricated.'

'Yes, quite.' Tel Varon wasn't able to keep the lack of conviction out of his voice. 'I have spoken to the children, thoroughly checked their statements. They were all verified by lie-detector.' He looked searchingly at Blake. 'That puts them beyond dispute.'

'I'm sure it does. The Administration has gone to an enormous amount of trouble. By setting up false charges they've even put themselves at risk. There must be a number of people involved who know the truth. The more who know, the greater the risk.' Blake said softly, 'Now why? Why would they take that chance?'

'There's no possible reason that I can think of,' said the young man, choosing not to meet Blake's eye.

'I know you've heard the evidence, but just for the moment believe that I'm innocent. Believe that.'

'Well ...'

'At first I thought they wanted to silence me because I was a witness to the murder of some twenty people. The only witness.'

'If they're as ruthless as you suggest, then why don't they simply eliminate you?'

3

'I couldn't understand that either,' Blake said, lowering his voice. 'It took a long time. Then I began to see it. Apparently I was something of a political figure – I've no memory of it myself, I'm only reporting what I've heard.'

Almost despite himself, Tel Varon felt a vague flicker of interest. He said, 'It's true that you had a considerable following, but then you publicly denounced the whole movement and pledged support to the Administration. I think there are still people who secretly believe you were coerced into that statement –'

'That's exactly it!' Blake said, his voice now imbued with a quiet urgency. 'My death would have reinforced those doubts. The same would have been true if I'd been charged with being at a proscribed political meeting. So instead, they trump up vile charges – vile enough to discredit me forever.'

His obvious sincerity began to awaken doubts in Tel Varon's mind. The young advocate sensed that perhaps there was more to this than he had supposed.

'If it were true,' he said slowly, 'well, you must realise the implication of what you are saying: it would mean there's corruption at the very highest level of the Administration –'

He was interrupted by a low beeping sound which attracted the attention of everyone in the court. The murmur of voices died away.

The clerk of the court rose to his feet. 'Now be silent,' he intoned solemnly. 'By the authority of the Administration this tribunal is now in session.'

Tel Varon and Alta Morag stepped forward to stand at the central desk, and a moment later the Arbiter entered through a side door and took his place, nodding to the clerk to start the proceedings.

'The Arbiter will permit submissions,' the clerk announced.

Returning to their respective desks, Tel Varon and Alta Morag each picked up a large canister of computer tape

34

and placed them before the Arbiter, then withdrew to their appointed positions.

'Let the accused be brought forward,' the Arbiter instructed, and Blake was led to a dais, which he mounted and faced the court. His face was pale yet composed.

The Arbiter leaned forward, pressing the tips of his fingers together. He waited a moment, and then said, 'Have you, the accused, been made aware of the charges that are laid against you, and do you fully understand the nature and gravity of those charges?'

Blake's voice was quiet and firm in the hushed courtroom. 'Yes.'

'Who speaks for the Administration?'

Alta Morag gave a slight bow. 'I.'

'Who speaks for the accused?'

Tel Varon did the same. 'I.'

'Are you both satisfied that the evidence used in preparing the prosecution tape was fairly obtained, and that all statements were certified as true and accurate by lie-detector?'

'I am,' Alta Morag asserted confidently.

Tel Varon glanced towards Blake. 'I am,' he said after a momentary hesitation.

'Is the accused satisfied that his defence has been fully and fairly prepared?' the Arbiter enquired in his clipped emotionless tone.

'The charges against me are totally false. I am not guilty, therefore I offer no defence.'

'Your guilt or innocence is what we are here to determine,' said the Arbiter imperturbably. 'If there are no further submissions the case will be examined.'

He reached out his hand to receive one of the canisters from the clerk, and held it up in full view.

'Let it be seen that the evidence for the prosecution is sealed and approved by the defence,' and so saying broke the heavy seal and took out the reel of tape, which he handed to

Alta Morag. Then he held aloft the second canister, and in the same flat voice, 'Let it be seen that the evidence for the defence is sealed and approved by the prosecution.'

Breaking the seal, he gave the tape to Tel Varon, who together with Alta Morag approached the computer on the far side of the room. The clerk took the two reels of tape and fitted them on to adjacent spindles, and the two legal representatives returned to their positions before the central desk.

The clerk waited, his finger hovering over the button, and it was as if, just for a moment, the courtroom was held suspended in a kind of breathless limbo.

Then the Arbiter pronounced, 'Let the matter be assessed and may justice prevail.'

The button was pressed, the reels spun, multi-coloured lights began to flash in sequence, and the subdued hum of electronic circuitry softly invaded the silence. Varon's tape was the first to finish and it was some time before the prosecution reel finally spun to a stop.

Everyone waited, their eyes fixed on the computer, and then as if suddenly coming alive the automatic typewriter began a rapid staccato chattering, the broad ribbon of paper jerking rapidly from the slot. The clerk waited impassively, and when the machine had finished tore off the printout and brought it to the Arbiter, who held it in both hands like a scroll and studied it for several moments.

He raised his head and stared directly at Blake. Then he spoke, his voice devoid of all emotion and expression:

'The accused has been found guilty on all charges. His crimes have been accorded a Category Nine rating and as such are adjudged most grave. In sentencing you, the Justice Machine has taken into account your past record, your service to the State and your loyalty to the Administration. None of these have mitigated in your favour. It is then the sentence of this tribunal that you be taken from this place to an area of close confinement. From there you will be transported to the Penal Colony on the planet Cygnus Alpha where you will remain for the rest of your natural life. This matter is ended.'

The Arbiter placed the printout on the desk and rose to his feet.

'I would like to speak,' Blake said, quietly yet distinctly.

'There can be no more said regarding this case,' the Arbiter informed him imperiously. 'The evidence has been assessed and judgement made.'

'But the evidence is false . . . the charges are false!'

'There was no proof of falsification of evidence in your defence tape,' said the Arbiter, preparing to move away.

Blake's voice thickened with anger and mounting desperation.

'Because I have no evidence! My only proof is my innocence!'

'If you have any complaint against the conduct of this tribunal, it must be directed through your counsel. That is all.'

The Arbiter turned away, his duty fulfilled, but before he had moved a couple of paces Blake had leapt forward, cleared the desk, and wrenched at his arm.

'Listen to me! You've got to listen to me!'

The entire courtroom had been stunned by this sudden and dramatic gesture, but in seconds it seemed that everyone had converged on Blake, hands clawing at him from every direction, and with absolutely ruthless efficiency the guards overpowered him and held him fast. One of them slipped a small pistol-like device from his holster, the gleaming point of a hypodermic needle protruding from the blunt snout, and pressed it against Blake's upper arm.

The high-concentration suppressant acted almost instantaneously and Blake felt his strength drain away, his legs buckling beneath him, so that he fell in an untidy heap, his vision fading as the drug affected the primary nerve-centres of the brain.

He was surrounded by legs, which seemed to rise to enormous heights, like trees in a forest, and his mind seized on odd inconsequential details: the scuff-marks on the floor, the frayed seam of a coverall, the soft cloth shoes.

Darkness closed in around him, and at the far end of what seemed a long black tunnel he could see a face staring down at him, a face he had seen somewhere before. Hazily, he struggled to remember . . . and then he knew.

It was the man with blond hair.

The bright circle of light flickered and dimmed and he was floating in the infinite blackness of outer space.

3

A pair of dexterous hands moved with practised ease through the pockets of the supine figure on the low concrete bench. Finding little of interest, they rapidly unfastened the digital chronometer from the man's wrist and in a trice it was gone, vanished into thin air, as if by sleight of hand.

Not a moment too soon, Vila Restal told himself, as the man's eyelids fluttered and he started to come round. Affecting a look of concern, Vila lightly slapped the man's face, leaning over him in the manner of an anxious friend.

Blake came slowly, painfully, back to reality. The face that greeted his return reminded him of a gargoyle. It was small, pinched, swarthy, and contained a pair of eyes that held a mischievous twinkle, despite their expression of apparently sincere concern.

'Who are you?' Blake mumbled through parched lips.

Vila tutted in mock annoyance. 'Wrong . . . I got it wrong!' he reprimanded himself, his head wagging from side to side. 'I bet myself your first words would be "Where am I?" But have it your own way.' He smiled brightly. 'My name is Vila.'

'Where are we?' Blake asked, struggling to sit up. His brain felt too large for his skull.

'Now that's better,' said the small, agile man, doing a little dance and spreading his arms wide like a conjuror about to present his greatest illusion. 'This, my friend, is the luxurious first-class transit lounge of the interplanetary launch complex, where the lucky passengers are pampered and cossetted until launch time.'

Blake looked around him groggily. At first he had the ridiculous notion that he was in a cage; he looked again and saw that he *was* in a cage. Three of the walls were made of metal mesh, the fourth a slab of rough concrete with a metal door set into it. The whole place was dank and unpleasant, illuminated by a single dim spotlight which threw a wash of insipid yellow over the littered floor, the low concrete benches, and, deeper in the gloom, several murky figures in various attitudes of bored indolence.

Where in hell was he? He looked up, confused, at the small man who stood before him. 'I don't understand.'

'All right,' said Vila Restal, ever the helpful guide. 'Then try this. We're in a transit cell. Through that door is a prison ship. As soon as she's fuelled we'll be loaded aboard and blasted off to spend the rest of our lives on Cygnus Alpha.'

The name of the planet brought it all back. 'The Penal Colony,' Blake said through numbed lips.

'Devil's Island in the sky!' Vila responded mockingly. 'The planet of no return.' He cocked his head to one side. 'You know how many people have escaped from there? None! Not one! Ever!'

'And why are you being sent there?' Blake enquired, more out of politeness than curiosity.

Vila smiled brightly. 'I steal things,' he said, completely unabashed. 'It's not my fault, you understand . . . I mean, it's compulsive, you know? Some of the best shrinks in the business have worked on my head, but I just go on taking things that don't belong to me.'

'A professional thief,' Blake observed quietly.

But Vila was quick to correct him. 'Oh no, it's not a profession,' he said, his dark eyes large and serious. 'More a vocation. I mean, I've elevated stealing into an art form – '

'Give the man his watch back.'

A girl was standing at Vila's shoulder. She was quite tall, slim, with dark hair, and even in the dim light Blake could see that she was extraordinarily beautiful. It took a moment for her words to register, and then he realised that his chronometer was missing.

With a movement that was almost too quick to perceive, Vila conjured up the chronometer out of nowhere and handed it back, totally without embarrassment.

'I was taking care of it while you were unconscious,' he explained solicitously. 'Some very bad people in here.'

Blake strapped the chronometer on to his wrist, nodding his thanks to the girl.

'This is Jenna,' said Vila offhandedly, glancing round the cage.

Blake introduced himself.

'What are you here for?' she asked him, her eyes cool, almost lazy in their scrutiny of him.

'I was set up –'

'But of *course* you were,' Vila said, his sympathy full of sardonic undertones. 'We all were. Every one of us is a victim of a miscarriage of justice.'

'I *was* set up,' Blake retorted with some fervour.

The girl nodded, humouring him as if he were a child. 'Sure . . . right . . . we believe you.'

Blake looked at the pair of them, realising the futility of trying to convince them. He shrugged and gestured towards the other prisoners in the cage. 'What about all the others? What have they done?'

'Don't mix with them,' Vila advised him darkly, lowering his voice. 'A very anti-social bunch. Murderers, smugglers, liars, cheats. And they're the nice ones.'

'All condemned to Cygnus?'

Jenna nodded.

'Just one big happy family,' Vila observed gleefully.

'How long before we take off?' Blake asked, a sudden feeling of disquiet making his tone urgent.

'About twenty-four hours,' Jenna answered.

'A day,' Blake said, half to himself. 'Just one day.'

Jenna regarded him with a mixture of mockery and cynical amusement.

'If you're expecting a last-minute reprieve, forget it. Once they get you this far there's no going back. Just get used to the idea. Nobody out there gives a damn about you.'

Maja Varon stirred restlessly in the large oval bed and half-opened her eyes, gazing sleepily towards the lighted doorway. She sighed and called out her husband's name, feeling rather irritable and wondering what was taking him so long.

He appeared in the doorway, still dressed, holding a drink.

'What time is it?' Maja yawned, stretching her limbs.

'Oneish,' Tel Varon replied, sipping his drink distractedly.

'Come to bed,' Maja implored him.

'I can't sleep.' Tel Varon looked unseeingly into the darkened room. 'There's something wrong but I just can't pin it down,' he said in a faraway voice.

'The Blake affair?'

Her husband nodded slowly. 'I didn't do my job today. I saw the prosecution evidence and it was so complete and so perfect that I accepted it. I just assumed Blake was guilty and concentrated on justification and appeals for mercy.'

'There wasn't much else you could do,' Maja pointed out, fully awake now. 'You interviewed the victims, the witnesses – none of them had any doubts.'

'Perhaps they should have had.'

She leaned up on one elbow. 'What do you mean?'

'I don't know, I'm grabbing at straws.' He looked into the bottom of his glass. 'Maybe Blake is guilty all the way, but even so I should have done my job better – '

Abruptly he finished off his drink, put the glass down, and

started to fasten his uniform. His manner was suddenly brisk, almost agitated.

'Where are you going?'

'The Public Records Computer.'

'To look for what?'

Tel Varon shrugged, fastening the top button. 'I don't know.'

'Give me a minute,' said Maja, getting quickly out of bed and reaching for her clothes. 'I'll come with you.'

The Computer Room of the Public Records Office was silent but not deserted. It was a strict rule that it was never left unattended, and even at this hour of the night the Duty Operator was required to maintain his vigil. He dozed fitfully under the bland concealed lighting, rousing himself reluctantly as Tel Varon and his wife appeared before his desk.

'Tel Varon, Justice Department.' The young man showed his identification. 'I want to run a check on these names,' he requested, holding out a list.

'It'll have to wait till morning,' the Duty Operator told him, massaging his left shoulder, deliberately ignoring the sheet of paper.

Tel Varon thrust it under his nose. 'I want it now.'

The Operator took it ungraciously and moved to the keyboard. With infuriating slowness he began to tap out the names from the list. Tel Varon glanced at his wife, controlling his impatience, and then looked towards the computer as it began to hum into electronic life. It took only seconds to retrieve the information from its vast memory data-bank and deliver it in the form of three typed plasticards. Tel Varon scooped them from the perspex tray and scanned them quickly, Maja peering over his shoulder.

'Nothing here,' he muttered. 'Admission to Clinic . . . treatment records . . . it all tallies with the evidence.'

He thought of something and turned to the Operator. 'Let me have the school attendance records on these three.'

The Operator punched some keys and after a rapid clicking of relays the computer spat out three more cards.

'That's interesting,' Tel Varon mused, reading the first card. 'This child was away from school on the afternoon before the assault.'

'And there's an absence marked on this one too,' Maja declared. 'Again it's just before the date.'

The couple exchanged glances and held the third plasticard up to the light.

Tel Varon breathed out slowly. 'Three makes it more than a coincidence. Now where were they on those days, I wonder?'

He frowned and began to pace up and down; suddenly he clicked his fingers and said to the Operator:

'Give me the admissions to the Central Clinic on those dates.'

The Operator gave an audible sigh and punched a series of keys. But this time no cards emerged, and instead the computer emitted a long steady beep and a red light flashed on the control panel.

'What's the matter with it?' Maja demanded.

'That means the information has been classified,' the Operator informed her, and then as if repeating instructions by rote, 'such information cannot be obtained without due authority from the Administration.'

'But I need it,' Tel Varon insisted.

The Operator shook his head adamantly. 'I'm sorry.'

'Er . . . look,' said Tel Varon, his voice adopting a gentler tone. 'The Justice Department can get an order made releasing that information – ' he was taking a billfold from his pocket ' – but it takes time and form-filling . . . '

He had peeled off three notes and was holding them up invitingly.

The Operator eyed them, rubbing his chin. 'This is strictly between ourselves,' he warned, taking them and tucking them away.

'Of course.'

The Operator pressed a key and the computer hummed into action. A moment later a single card lay in the perspex tray. Tel Varon snatched it up.

'Look at that – the date!' He read from the card, ' "Outpatient admission: identity unrecorded". And this one too –'

'Three unidentified admissions on the dates the victims weren't at school,' Maja said excitedly.

'It's not foolproof yet but it gives us somewhere to start,' Tel Varon said, a determined glint appearing in his eyes.

'But why would they have been to the Clinic?' Maja wanted to know.

'I can't be certain, but try this for a start. Mental implantation.'

'What's that?'

'Creating a fictional experience and emotion and implanting them into the mind of the subject so vividly and permanently that they become reality.'

Maja stared at him. 'Is it possible?'

'Oh yes,' said her husband grimly. 'The process was perfected years ago but then outlawed by the medical profession.' He looked at her, his expression brooding and serious. 'But if it's being used again . . . '

'You could prove Blake's innocence.'

'And blow the top off the whole Administration.' He took her arm. 'Come on.'

'Where are we going?'

'I've got to talk to Blake,' said Tel Varon, heading with single-minded determination for the door.

The Duty Operator waited until they had gone, then unhurriedly, almost casually, pressed a short sequence of buttons on the audiophone. The connection was made instantly.

He smoothed his pocket, feeling the folded bulge of notes, and said softly:

'Security?'

*

Complete privacy was out of the question in the cramped confines of the transit cage, so they had to make do with a gloomy corner, the three of them huddled together like conspirators. Blake had been overjoyed to see them, though now he was sweating as Tel Varon pressed him to remember every tiny detail of what had taken place the night of the massacre.

'The cave . . . how did you get to it?'

Blake screwed his eyes shut and fought to piece his scattered thoughts together. 'I can't be sure. It was dark.'

'Come on. This is vital.' Tel Varon stared into Blake's tortured face. 'Which exit did you use?'

'Sub-43.'

'Sub-43,' Tel Varon repeated, his thoughts racing. 'That would be on the northern perimeter of the Dome. All right. Where did you go then?'

Blake opened his eyes and gazed unseeingly into the dimness. The other prisoners were clustered together in small groups on the far side of the cage, straining to hear what was being said. They were intrigued as to the purpose of this visit, and rather envious too.

Blake began slowly, 'It was fairly rocky country. We seemed to travel about three miles. Not too far from the cave there was a spring, a small stream in the rocks.'

'That should help,' Maja said hopefully.

'We'll find it,' Tel Varon asserted with conviction. 'Now, is there anything else you can remember . . . anything at all?'

'A face.' Blake spoke as if in a trance. 'A man's face.'

'What man?'

'He was in the court today. I – I caught a glimpse of him just before I became unconscious.'

'What about him?' Maja asked, leaning closer.

'I've seen him before somewhere . . . ' Blake stared blankly ahead, picturing the face in his mind's eye. Where had he seen –

'He was in the cave! That's where I saw him!' He snapped

his fingers as his memory cleared, like a beam of sunlight breaking through the clouds. 'I thought he was one of us but it must have been him who gave the signal. He betrayed them – it was him!'

'What did he look like?' Tel Varon asked intently.

'He's very blond – almost an albino – with extremely shifty eyes. And he's got quite a pronounced limp.'

'Tarrant,' said Tel Varon at once.

'Who's he?'

'He's in Security. Works in the outer systems most of the time. Undercover, I think –'

'He's a murderer. I'll find him somehow.'

'If I can get the evidence I want, you won't need to,' Tel Varon assured him firmly. His expression was sober, utterly determined. 'He'll come to trial like everybody else in this cover-up.'

'What do you plan on doing?'

'First, I'm going to talk to my Head of Department, get a holding order on you. At least you can stay here on Earth while we investigate. Then, if I can find this cave I'll have enough evidence for a full enquiry.'

'You don't have much time,' Blake said with a note of anxiety.

'I'll get started on it now.' Tel Varon rose quickly to his feet. He tried to give what reassurance he could. 'With luck you'll be taken back to the city detention area within a couple of hours.'

Blake stood up and held out his hand. 'Thanks.'

Tel Varon responded somewhat uncomfortably. 'Listen, I didn't believe you before . . . I should have done more. I'm sorry.'

'You're doing it now,' Blake told the younger man gratefully.

'Yes. I'll be in touch.' He gave a final brief smile and he and his wife left the transit cage, leaving Blake in a much happier frame of mind.

Vila sauntered over, hands tucked in his pockets as if he were taking a Sunday afternoon stroll. 'Friends in high places, eh?' he said casually. 'Can't you put in a word for us?'

'Be glad to,' Blake grinned.

'You're leaving us, are you?' Jenna Stannis said, appraising him coolly. 'Just when we were getting to know one another . . .'

'It would break my heart,' said Blake, shaking his head sadly. 'I mean, I was really looking forward to spending the rest of my life on Cygnus.' He cocked an eyebrow. 'You never did tell me what you were charged with.'

Jenna shrugged dismissively. 'Smuggling. They claimed I was trading around the near systems in prohibited cargoes.'

'And were you?'

'Certainly not!' Jenna replied, affronted. She sniffed and glanced away. 'Well . . . maybe just a little,' she amended.

'Oh, come on now,' Vila said, nudging her slyly. 'They've been trying to nail you down for years.' He winked at Blake. 'She's just being modest. She's a pretty big name – what you might call the criminal's criminal.'

'Those were the days,' Jenna sighed wistfully.

A harsh metallic voice grated from the speaker overhead, rupturing the silence:

'Attention! Attention! Launch time has been advanced to seventeen hundred hours. Embarkation will commence at sixteen hundred hours. That is all.'

'That's just eight hours away,' Blake said, glancing nervously at his chronometer. He looked perturbed.

'Now I wonder what that's about?' Vila mused aloud, his small, swarthy face crinkling in puzzlement. 'Why the sudden hurry?'

Blake wondered too, though he had a pretty shrewd idea.

*

Tel Varon stood before Ven Glynd's desk, conscious of the fact that every minute counted if he was going to prevent a grave miscarriage of justice. He was now more than ever convinced that Blake's story was substantially true, and his voice betrayed the urgency of his appeal.

'I think that on what I have learned already there is strong evidence of conspiracy,' he told the large man who sat comfortably at ease. Even at this late hour his grooming was impeccable, not a hair out of place.

'Not strong evidence,' Glynd qualified, 'but enough, I think, to raise reasonable doubt.'

'Then you'll order an enquiry?'

'Naturally.' Glynd nodded gravely. 'The whole matter will have to be investigated.'

Tel Varon released a sudden breath and his manner relaxed slightly. 'Good,' he said, relieved. 'Thank you.'

'You look as though you could use some sleep. You've had a busy night.'

'I'm all right,' Tel Varon declared, happier now and impatient for action. 'I'd like an authority to go outside the Dome.'

'This cave business, you mean.' Glynd waved his well-padded hands as if it were a minor matter easily dealt with. 'There's no need for you to do it. I'll have a team make a survey of the area you described. If they find anything I'll advise you right away.'

'All right,' Tel Varon agreed reluctantly. 'And the holding order to return Blake to the city?'

'I'll take care of everything,' Van Glynd assured him smoothly. He got to his feet, grunting with the effort. 'Now off you go and get some rest, you've done more than your share.'

The young man nodded dutifully and left the office, satisfied now that the wheels had been set in motion: but it had been a close thing.

Maja was waiting anxiously for him in the corridor and

straight away he set her mind at ease. 'It's going to be all right,' he said, smiling, and embraced her.

Before he could explain further, the slightly muffled voice of Ven Glynd reached them through the transom above the door:

'Link me with Dr Havant at the Central Clinic.'

Tel Varon went quite still and raised a warning finger to his lips. He moved closer, his head inclined to one side to catch Glynd's next words:

'Havant? I think we may have a little problem . . . yes, that's right . . . For the moment it would be best if you were, shall we say, unavailable . . . No, no, nothing that can't be handled from this end, just a few little loopholes that need to be closed. In a day or so everything will be tidied up . . . Yes, that's about it . . . '

Maja gripped her husband's hand, suddenly afraid. They stared at one another, horrified, as Glynd finished the conversation.

'Yes, arrange to take calls only directly from me . . . Fine . . . Good-bye.'

They heard him break the connection and then the muffled sound of a cough.

Tel Varon led his wife quickly along the corridor, and it was only when they had turned a corner that they felt it safe to speak.

'What does it mean?' Maja implored him, her eyebrows drawn together.

'It's obvious, isn't it?' Tel Varon spoke bitterly, a dull flush of anger rising in his cheeks. 'Glynd is involved. He's part of it.'

'Then where do we go from here?'

'Higher up,' said her husband curtly. 'The President if we have to.'

'Then let's try and arrange to see him – now. There's not much time.'

'We'll need a whole lot more evidence before we can do

that,' Tel Varon said, gnawing at a thumbnail. 'If we're going to make accusations against Glynd we'll need a watertight case.' He glanced along the corridor. 'Here, I want to try something – '

He strode across to an audiophone mounted on the wall, lifted the handset and gave it to Maja. 'I'm getting the Clinic,' he told her as he punched a series of numbers. 'Ask for Dr Havant, tell them it's Ven Glynd.'

His wife nodded, showing she understood, and moistened her lips nervously. The connection was made and she said at once, 'Hello? Dr Havant, please. Ven Glynd calling . . . Dr Havant, I have Ven Glynd for you.'

She passed the handset to Tel Varon, who spoke quickly and confidently, lowering his voice in what was a creditable imitation of Glynd's gruff tones.

'Sorry to call you again. Something I forgot. Are there any clinical records about this matter . . . treatment charts, medical notes, anything of that kind?'

He listened for a moment. Then, authoritatively:

'Right, I think I'd better have them. Put them in an envelope and leave them at reception. I'll have them picked up. Good-bye.'

He replaced the handset, his eyes lighting up triumphantly. 'We've got them! Look, you go to the Clinic and pick up the envelope. Then go home and collect the tape-camera.'

'Where are you going?'

Tel Varon allowed himself a brief tense smile. 'To talk to a thief I once defended. He should be able to get me a lock-pick.' He checked his chronometer. 'I'll meet you in about two hours at Sub-43.' He gripped her hand tightly. 'We're going Outside.'

Blake was in a fever of impatience. He drummed his fingers against the metal mesh of the cage, staring beyond into the empty darkness. Thoughts seemed to whirl in his brain in a dizzying spiral so that it was impossible to concentrate for more than a few seconds on any one thing. And he had looked at his wrist chronometer so many times that its illuminated display appeared to him like a meaningless hieroglyph.

From the corner of his eye he became vaguely aware that Jenna was silently watching him. She drifted across; he admired her calmness and self-possession. She seemed indifferent to her fate.

'Not long now,' she murmured, studying his worried face in the dim light.

'They've had enough time to issue a holding order.' Blake spoke inwardly, carrying on an anguished dialogue with himself. 'It should have been here by now.'

'These things always take time.' Her voice was quietly reassuring. 'People to see, forms to fill out . . . don't worry, they'll get it here.'

They shared a moment of gloomy silence, both wrapped in their own thoughts. When next she spoke, Jenna's voice had dropped to little more than a whisper.

'I wish somebody was working to let me stay here. Until now it hasn't been real . . . I didn't let myself believe it was happening. But now it's so close, I'm scared.'

Blake looked at her, realising for the first time what she must be going through. Her cool indifference was a brave front, little more than skin deep.

Once again he checked the time, the frustration building up in him like an explosive mixture of gas. *Where the hell were they?*

As Maja came down the stairway, her footsteps echoing flatly from the rough concrete walls of the basement, Tel Varon appeared out of the shadows.

'Did you get everything?'

She nodded, showing him the envelope and the tape-camera in its vinyl case.

'Good.' He was well pleased. 'Let me see that.' He took the envelope, slit it open, and leafed through the various documents. His delighted grin confirmed that this was the evidence they required. 'It's all here. We could build a case on this alone.'

'Did you get what you wanted?'

Tel Varon held up the Vibra lock-pick. He went across to the door and began to operate the instrument as he had been instructed.

'I've never been Outside,' Maja whispered, watching her husband as he scanned the lock with the small black device.

'I did. Once. Years ago. It's very strange. I didn't like it.'

There came the faintest of clicks, barely audible, and Tel Varon gripped the handle and slowly turned it. The door opened.

A single red warning light came on: security alert.

A relay chattered into life and just as abruptly stopped.

The computer was silent once more.

The Operator took the small oblong plasti-card from the tray and went immediately to the console, punched numbers on the audiophone panel, and spoke in a low voice empty of all expression:

'Computer registers an unauthorised opening of the door at Sub-43.'

Her eyes were sharper than his and so she was the first to see the darker area of black against the sheer cliff-face.

'Look!' Maja said eagerly. 'There . . .'

Tel Varon laid a restraining hand on her shoulder. 'You wait here a minute.'

He advanced cautiously, swallowed up in the darkness,

and Maja listened to the sound of his fading footsteps. She hugged herself, not from cold, but rather as if seeking comfort from bodily contact, even though it was her own. There was something ominous and evil about this place, her senses told her so as plainly as if she had witnessed some dreadful event with her own eyes. She shivered and waited, peering ahead into the gloom.

Sooner than she expected Tel reappeared from the entrance of the cavern. His face bore an expression she couldn't remember ever having seen before; he looked ill, his eyes shocked, disbelieving. He said haltingly:

'What Blake told us . . . was true.'

Maja stepped forward but he barred her way.

'No.' Tel Varon shook his head emphatically. 'You stay outside. I'll search the bodies and take some picture tapes.'

He returned to the cavern, taking the camera from its case, and braced himself to face once again the scene of carnage. Raising the camera with its built-in flashlight, he began, systematically and with cold deliberation, to take pictures.

Bolts were drawn back and the metal door in the concrete wall flung open. Blake got hastily to his feet, smiling with relief, but the smile faded into a look of helpless dismay as the two guards, sidearms drawn, stood either side of the door, gesturing to the prisoners to stand up.

'You'll move out of here in single file and into the embarkation channel. All right, let's get started. Come on, move!'

One of the guards stepped forward, prodding the prisoners with his para-handgun. 'Come on, all of you, move!'

A shuffling line formed and started to file out.

The guard spotted Blake standing alone in a corner and thrust him forward. 'You – move into line!'

Jenna looked towards him, her eyes sad, sharing his despair, and then she too was hustled from the transit cage.

They were marched along a dim corridor, their footsteps echoing dully in the confined space, then up a concrete ramp and into a long narrow tubular compartment with padded seats either side of a central gangway.

Judging from its bleak, utilitarian appearance, this was one of the older spacecraft, equipped with nothing but the barest essentials for passenger survival. It certainly hadn't been designed for comfort.

Blake slid into a seat by one of the circular observation ports, peering out anxiously. There was still time, he told himself, making himself believe it; the holding order could still come through.

'How long before take-off?' he asked one of the guards.

'Forty-five minutes.' The guard gave a sneering grin. 'Why, you in a hurry to get there?'

Blake ignored him, staring out into the darkness.

At that same moment, just three miles from the northern perimeter of the Dome, Tel Varon and Maja were preparing to return to the city. The young man was sickened and exhausted by what he had seen; he fastened the tape-camera into its vinyl case, his fingers trembling with weariness and disgust.

'I've got everything we need,' he said quietly, controlling his voice.

'Enough to keep Blake here on Earth?'

'More than enough. Now they can't refuse to listen. But we'll have to hurry,' he said, slinging the camera across his shoulder and reaching for his wife's hand. Together they hurried back in the direction of the city.

'Fasten harnesses!'

The guard moved along the central gangway, checking that everyone was securely strapped down. The compartment vibrated from the low idling throb of the engines, a pulsing beat of sound that seemed almost malevolent.

The guard came alongside Blake, whose abstracted gaze was focused unblinkingly on the darkness beyond the port.

'What is it with you?' the guard demanded harshly. 'You want to be different to everybody else? I said fasten harnesses!'

Blake looked up, startled and uncertain. His thoughts had been a million miles away. 'I'm sorry . . . I didn't hear what you said.'

'Maybe we can help you to hear better,' the guard snarled. 'You can start the journey with a couple of hours' close confinement. You'll be surprised how good your hearing gets.' He barked suddenly, 'Arms on the rests! Head back!'

As Blake obeyed the command the guard called along the compartment. 'Seat eleven. Put him on CC.'

Curved metal clamps shot out of the arm-rests and closed over Blake's wrists. Another larger one swung from the rear of the seat, pinning his chest and shoulders, so that he was held fast, unable to move.

The guard curled his lip in a satisfied smirk and moved along, and just then the engines took on a higher note, slowly building up to full power in readiness for take-off.

The two figures to the north of the Dome glanced up as the bright flare of light lifted into the night sky. It rose slowly, seeming to hang against the backcloth of stars, and then gathered speed, the roar of its engines reverberating as the shock-waves of sound reached their ears.

In seconds it had diminished to a moving speck of light, not much brighter than the surrounding stars, and the sound had died away so that it was lost in the faint sighing of the breeze.

The shorter, broader of the two figures watched the fading pinpoint of light with evident satisfaction. 'There's an end to it,' said Tarrant softly.

He turned away, and then – almost as an afterthought – said to the guard:

'Oh, by the way . . . I think a transporter accident.' He nodded seriously. 'Killed instantly. Very tragic. Take care of it, will you?'

And, without a backward glance, he began to descend the rocky slope on which were sprawled the bodies of Tel and Maja Varon. There was no need to look back: he had made sure they were quite dead.

It was a beautiful, awe-inspiring sight, and yet for Blake the saddest thing he had ever seen: the planet Earth in all its blue-green splendour growing smaller and smaller as the spacecraft accelerated deep into space.

The guard leaned across, his face twisted with malicious pleasure. 'That's right, take a long look. It's the last you'll ever see of it.'

Blake turned from the observation port, and there was a certain look in his eyes that made the guard draw back a little.

Blake shook his head. 'No, I'm coming back,' he said very quietly. There wasn't any doubt left in him, only total and absolute conviction. 'Somehow, I'm coming back.'

4

The Civil Administration Space Vessel *London* had seen many worlds and better days. Unkindly described by one of its crew as 'an old interplanetary tub ready for the breaker's yard', it was certainly true that the titanium hull – streaked by burnt rocket gases and pitted with meteorite scars – had long since lost the shining bloom of youth. But it still had its certificate of space-worthiness, and so had been relegated to the lowly duty of ferrying political prisoners and other undesirables to the outer systems.

Commander Leylan knew just how the ship felt. He too was past his prime, having spent over thirty years in the service, and had evolved the philosophy that if he didn't hassle the Administration, the Administration wouldn't hassle him – which in his book meant doing his job, keeping his nose clean and turning a blind eye to things that didn't concern him. Such as who comprised his human cargo and why they were being shipped to the hell-hole of Cygnus Alpha.

Sitting at the Command Desk, he watched his crew go about the business of preparing the spacecraft for TDF – Time Distortion Function – which would accelerate the vessel from the escape velocity of 25,000 miles an hour to its deep space cruising speed. There was nothing for him to do except listen with half an ear as his number two, Sub-

Commander Raiker, and Flight Operator Artix went through the prelim checks with the bored confidence of a familiar routine.

Raiker was seated next to him, scanning the master instrument panel, his powerful, well-built frame hunched forward in an attitude that verged on the point of indolence. His flat, bored voice confirmed the impression.

'We have escape velocity . . . now.'

'Orbital exit angle, thirty degrees,' Artix responded.

'Set attitude and course trajectory.'

'Attitude stable. Trajectory firm.'

'Systems check,' Raiker requested.

Artix carried out a quick reading. 'We have full function on all navigational systems.'

'Confirmed.'

'We have full function on all communication systems.'

'Confirmed. Power status?'

'We have full function.' Artix reached forward to adjust a control. 'Course is set and locked on to Mars beacon.'

Raiker turned to the Captain. 'We have OK confirmation on all systems, sir.'

Leylan stirred himself. 'Thank you, Mister Raiker,' he said in his slow gentle voice. 'Set at a speed of Time-Distort Five.'

'Time-Distort Five,' acknowledged Raiker in the same flat, slightly nasal tone.

He took hold of a large red stirrup-like control set in the panel before him and drew it slowly back. The needle in the corresponding gauge crept from zero to five and at once the Fight Deck was shaken by a heavy vibration. The Flight personnel were pressed back into their seats and several loose objects skittered across the Command Desk and fell to the floor.

Gradually the vibration died away as the vessel attained its standard cruising speed. Raiker checked his instruments and reported:

'Five and running.'

Commander Leylan eased himself out of his seat and flexed his shoulders. 'Lock on to auto.' He said casually, 'I thought Maintenance were supposed to have straightened out that speed stress vibration?'

'They said they had,' shrugged Raiker.

'That's what they always say. I don't think they bother. They hope they can get away with a quick routine servicing.' He sighed, long past the stage of becoming irritated by such trifles, and nodded to Artix. 'You'd better identify us to Space Security.'

The young Flight Operator raised his eyebrows alertly. 'Yes, sir.' He was still fresh enough and new enough to the Service to take his duties seriously. He pressed a button and spoke in the regulation clipped tone that the manual insisted on for space communication:

'This is Civil Administration ship *London*. We are in transit from Earth to Cygnus Alpha, transporting prisoners to the Penal Colony. We have Administration clearance for direct flight. Authority number K-711. Transmission ends.'

He broke the connection and leaned back in his chair, a small happy smile on his face, and became aware that Commander Leylan was looking at him with furrowed brows, his gaze puzzled and slightly suspicious.

'What's the matter with your face, Artix?'

Artix rubbed his chin, embarrassed, and gave a sheepish grin. He hadn't shaved for over a week and the growth was fairly pronounced. He cleared his throat and said cautiously, 'I thought I might try a beard, but all it does is itch at the moment.'

Leylan frowned at his junior officer. 'If you were serving on one of the Federation Deep Space ships you'd have to ask the commander's permission.'

'Do you mind, sir?'

Leylan shook his head. 'You can grow it down to your

knees if you want to,' he said indifferently. 'I'm going to my quarters. Anything I should know?'

Artix glanced at the Met Chart. 'There's a report of some meteorite activity about eighteen Earth hours ahead. Space Met says it should have cleared our course well before we reach it.'

'All right, but keep an eye on it.' Leylan turned to his number two.

'Mister Raiker, will you give the prisoners the usual pep talk and assign them their duties?'

'My pleasure.' The Sub-Commander slid out from behind the Command Desk and straightened up. He had the easy arrogant stance of someone who believed himself better and more able than anyone he had ever met and was ever likely to – including Commander Leylan.

The two men left the Flight Deck together and walked without speaking towards Leylan's quarters. There was nothing lost between them in this lack of conversation: the one old and weary, counting the few remaining years before retirement; the other hard, younger, never missing a chance to demonstrate his superiority. And never letting a waking moment go by when he wasn't thinking of promotion, the opportunity to be rid of this rusty old bucket once and for all.

'Use the highest level of suppressants in the prisoners' rations,' Leylan ordered, halting at the door to his quarters. 'I like them docile.'

'Yes sir.'

The Captain pressed the palm of his hand against a rectangular panel of glowing blue perspex by the side of the cabin door, and the door, activated by his handprint, slid silently open. He stepped inside and then paused, calling out, 'Oh, Mister Raiker.'

'Sir?'

Leylan regarded his number two for a moment. 'There's a female prisoner on our manifest.'

Raiker's face was impassive. 'I had noticed that, sir.'

'Yes, well . . . be discreet.'

Raiker's eyes were mocking. 'Yes sir.'

The two men exchanged a look and Raiker continued on his way. The old man was a stickler for rules and regulations, he thought contemptuously. What the hell did it matter how the prisoners were treated? They were being deported to the Penal Colony, which meant that as far as the Administration were concerned they had ceased to exist.

He pressed his hand against the blue panel and went through into the passenger compartment. The guard at the door came grudgingly to attention as Raiker surveyed the prisoners, still strapped into their seats. He stood, legs braced apart, and proceeded to give them the standard briefing:

'I'm Sub-Commander Raiker and I think there are a few things you should know. The flight to Cygnus Alpha will take eight months. During that time you will obey every order or instruction that is given you. There is a punishment scale for infractions: it starts with long periods of confinement in your launch seat and ends with the Commander's right to order execution. If you have any complaints, I don't want to hear them. Understand this clearly . . . you have no rights whatsoever. None! Questions?'

The prisoners remained silent, none of them venturing to invoke the Sub-Commander's displeasure at this early stage of the journey; in any case, it was perfectly clear where they stood. Nowhere.

Raiker nodded once, abruptly, apparently satisfied with the lack of response, and issued a curt instruction to the guard.

'Open it up.'

In some respects it was like a clever stage illusion, for as the guard operated a control, the entire front bulkhead folded back on itself to reveal a much larger area – in effect an extension of the passenger compartment – containing tables, chairs and bunks all built-in to the structure of the ship. At the far end a door gave access to the rest of the vessel, which as Raiker was quick to point out was strictly out-of-bounds.

'This is the limit of your world from now on,' he said, jerking his thumb at the extended space. 'It has mess facilities, sleeping bays and a recreation area. Sort it out among yourselves how you use it. There are other rules,' he added, his eyes flat and cold. 'You'll find out what they are when you break them. That's all. Clear your harnesses, you're at liberty to move.'

The prisoners gratefully released themselves and stood up, stretching their cramped limbs. All except Blake, who was still pinned in his seat by the curved steel bands. Raiker noticed this and sauntered across, standing in front of him, hands on hips.

'You got yourself in trouble already?'

'I didn't hear an order.'

'You didn't hear an order – sir.'

Blake stared at him, then slowly nodded.

This wasn't enough for the Sub-Commander. 'Say it,' he demanded.

'I didn't hear an order. Sir.'

'What's your name?'

'Blake.'

Raiker reacted with surprise. 'So you're Blake,' he said, his mouth twisting in a snide grin. 'You made quite a name for yourself a few years back. Quite a celebrity. Something of a come-down isn't it? What was it they got you on? You molested some kids, didn't you?'

'The charges were fabricated –'

'Oh yeah, sure . . . well let me tell you something, Blake. You're nothing special as far as I'm concerned. You're just another piece of cargo. Remember that and you'll have no trouble. Understand?'

'I understand,' Blake said. 'Sir.'

Raiker gave his superior bullying grin. 'Good . . . you're

learning.' He called to the guard, 'Let him clear.'

A moment later the metal bands snapped back into the seat, leaving Blake free to move. He got slowly to his feet, rubbing his wrists, staring after Sub-Commander Raiker, who had wandered up forward to where Jenna was talking to Vila and another prisoner.

Raiker halted near the bulkhead, arms folded, and took his time inspecting her, letting his eyes linger over her slim young body. Then he pointed a finger at her and slowly crooked it. When she came across, unhurriedly, to join him, he asked her name; Jenna told him what it was, and Raiker said in an undertone :

'There are no special facilities for female prisoners on board this ship . . . ' There was a hint of slyness in his voice as he went on, 'But if you find conditions too difficult, I . . . er, I might be able to arrange something more comfortable . . . '

Jenna gazed up at him, her expression demure, and gave him a simpering smile. 'That's very considerate of you.'

'Might as well make it easy on yourself,' Raiker said silkily, staring directly into her eyes.

'Thank you,' Jenna replied with heartfelt gratitude.

She looked quickly from side to side, as if not wishing to be overheard, and with a sultry smile beckoned him closer. Raiker bent forward to hear her whispered proposal, his face smug with the knowledge of conquest, and the expression slowly froze over and stiffened into incredulity, followed by blazing uncontrollable anger. He jerked his head back and stared into Jenna's sweetly smiling face. Then with the full sweep of his arm struck her hard across the cheek, turned on his heel and went out.

Jenna watched him go, gently rubbing her stinging face, and rejoined Vila and the other prisoner, who was called Kerr Avon. 'This one is going to enjoy giving us a hard time,' she told them thoughtfully.

Vila's attention had been caught by Blake, who was standing nearby, examining the rectangular blue panel at the side of the door.

'What are you doing?' Vila asked curiously, peering over his shoulder.

'Trying to figure out how these door panels work,' Blake replied, tracing the smooth surface of the panel with his fingertips.

'It's very simple,' said Kerr Avon, who spoke with such knowing authority that Blake glanced up, rather surprised. He saw a man with large pale eyes and a high domed forehead, who at a guess was somewhere in his thirties.

The man went on confidently, 'All authorised personnel have their palm prints filed on the computer. The blue sensor plate reads the print. If they conform, the computer opens the door.'

'You know that for certain?' Blake asked, regarding Kerr Avon with a measure of respect.

'He should,' Vila interjected. 'When it comes to computers he's the number two man in the world.'

'Who's the number one?'

'The guy who caught him,' said Vila with a cheeky grin, not at all put out by the withering look the man shot in his direction. 'You've got nothing to be ashamed of,' he said, then to Blake, 'He came damn close to stealing five million credits out of the Federation banking system.'

'What happened?' Blake asked, his interest aroused.

'The other people let me down,' Kerr Avon said shortly, obviously not prepared to go into detail. He seemed to regard himself as a cut above the others, no doubt thinking of them as small fry in the criminal stakes, and even when Jenna introduced Blake he seemed unimpressed, merely nodded distantly.

The group moved away from the door, and Blake said to Jenna, 'Know anything about this type of ship?'

She shrugged. 'Not a lot. It's a converted space trader,

5

about fifty years old I should think. Slow – not very sophisticated – but reliable.'

'Could you fly it?' Blake enquired casually.

'Fly it?' Jenna frowned at him. 'The only things I've ever flown are close space craft. I've never handled anything this big.'

'But could you?' Blake persisted.

'Well, I . . . ' Jenna wasn't too sure, but after a moment's consideration she admitted, 'I suppose so. Why do you want to know?'

Blake said calmly, 'We'll need a pilot when we take over the ship,' and moved on leaving the three of them looking after him in blank astonishment.

'There shouldn't be anything there at all!'

Commander Leylan swept his hand over the navigational star chart which was spread across the Command Desk. 'It's empty space,' he declared irritably. 'Nothing orbits through it. No marked space wrecks, no navigational hazards . . . nothing.'

'Well, there's something there now,' Artix replied, fingering what had flourished into a respectable beard instead of the original unsightly growth. 'And our course takes us right through it.'

They had long ago passed beyond the solar system and were now in deep space, in a region that on all the charts was a featureless waste. So why wasn't it? Leylan asked himself gloomily. He had made this trip at least a dozen times and had never encountered so much as a stray asteroid.

Sub-Commander Raiker came on to the Flight Deck and in that same instant a tremor passed swiftly through the ship. It was quite brief, lasting only a second or two, but strong enough to make everyone grab for the nearest anchored support. It was accompanied by a sound like that of stones rattling against the hull.

'What was that?' Raiker asked sharply, holding on to the rail which circled the Command Desk.

'Shock waves,' Leylan replied briskly. 'We had one about ten minutes ago, but it was only Force Two. We hardly noticed it. What was the reading on that?' he asked his junior officer.

Artix checked a gauge. 'Force Seven.'

'There could be more coming,' Leylan said grimly. 'Advise all sections to batten down and observe turbulance conditions. There's obviously some debris in the blast too. Put out the deflector shields.'

Artix moved to the microphone and began advising the crew of the situation, while Raiker went to his position at the Desk and deftly operated a sequence of controls that he obviously knew by heart.

'Deflectors out,' he reported. 'Where's the blast coming from?'

Leylan circled an area on the chart. 'Somewhere in this sector.'

Raiker glanced across. 'But that's total void.'

'Not now it isn't.' Leylan nodded to Artix. 'Show him.'

The Flight Operator brought the long-range electronic scanner to life and the three officers clustered round the screen.

'I never saw anything like that before,' said Raiker, watching the graceful curve and interplay of several light tracers. They wove together in a complex, delicate pattern, beautiful in its ever-changing symmetry. 'Can you get greater magnification?'

'No, we're on maximum.'

'What sort of range?'

'About a quarter of a mill,' said Leylan, the lines on his face more pronounced as he studied the display, looking all of his fifty-five years.

'Anything coming in on the communicators?'

Artix shook his head. 'Static right across the range,' he said tersely.

Raiker was nonplussed. 'I suppose it could be some sort of meteorite collision,' he ventured tentatively.

Their attention was taken by one of the speeding tracers, which all of a sudden expanded into a glowing ball of white, then instantly disappeared, its image wiped from the screen.

'What happened there?' Artix said, wide-eyed.

'That's it!' Leylan exclaimed. He thumped his fist against the console. 'That's all it can be – a damn great space battle with two fleets . . . maybe more!'

'I think you've got it,' Raiker agreed. 'It's the only thing that makes sense.'

'But we don't have any battle cruisers in this section,' Artix objected.

'No, they're not Federation ships,' Leylan asserted positively. 'And it's not our battle, so we're not going near it. Artix, I want a new course. Take us round it with a quarter mill margin from the outer limits of the action.'

Artix began punching buttons on his navigation computer, feeding in new data. Just then another shock wave hit the vessel, stronger this time and more sustained, and the hull clanged and reverberated with the rattle of debris.

'What was the reading?' Leylan demanded, his face tense, his mouth a hard straight line.

'Force Nine,' Raiker responded crisply. He looked up and met the Captain's eye. 'If you shift course now we'll be taking those blasts broadside. They'll knock the hell out of us.'

'Would you rather end up in the middle of a war?' Leylan became decisive, his long experience standing him in good stead when the situation demanded it. 'Take the controls, Mister Raiker. Artix, put the ship on full emergency. All crew to operational stations!'

At his command the Flight personnel went quickly and efficiently about their tasks, preparing the ship for a change of course. Every man knew that his life depended on how well he performed his duties: discipline was everything under deep space conditions.

As the computer began to relay the new flight trajectory, another tremor rocked the ship, more prolonged than before, and this time far more violent.

Blake was in the worst possible position to receive such a shock wave – tightly wedged in the narrow space between the outer hull and the inner wall of the ship. This double skin was designed to serve two purposes: as a barrier against meteorite penetration, and as a channel for the intricate network of cables and transducers linking each part of the vessel's control and communication systems.

Thick skeins of multi-coloured cables were clamped to the inner bulkhead, leaving barely enough room to squeeze past, and as the ship rocked under the impact of the tremor, Blake's head was flung sideways against the sharp projecting rim of a stanchion. In the same moment the hull was bombarded with fragments, clanging loudly in the conduit channel with the sharpness of high-velocity reports.

Squirming down, Blake managed to reach out and rap lightly on an inspection panel, then waited in the cramped darkness, feeling the slow trickle of blood down his forehead.

Standing with her back to the inspection cover, Jenna heard the signal and immediately put the plan into operation. She nodded to Olag Gan, a tall, powerfully-built young man who strolled unhurriedly across to a group of prisoners, leading them into the centre of the passenger compartment to form a screen between the inspection cover and the guard, effectively blocking his line of vision. Meanwhile, Vila had begun to perform a neat hand trick, claiming the guard's attention.

The whole thing was carried out with the casual, deceptive ease of an operation that has been planned down to the smallest detail and executed with split-second timing.

Then came the crucial moment. Making sure that the guard couldn't possibly see, Jenna and Kerr Avon knelt down and quickly unfastened the retaining bolts on the inspection cover, removed it and helped Blake squeeze out; they replaced the cover and straightened up, nodding to Olag Gan and Vila to tell them that everything was okay and the ploy had worked.

Vila completed his trick with a flourish, and with Olag drifted back to the small group by the rear bulkhead. Everything was back to normal.

'You're hurt,' Jenna said, seeing the cut on Blake's forehead.

He brushed it aside, too excited to concern himself with such a minor accident. 'Banged about a bit in the turbulence,' he said briefly, then looked round the circle of intent faces. 'I got past both metal grilles this time,' an admission which evoked guarded nods of satisfaction.

'You were right, Avon,' Blake went on, keeping his voice low. 'The wiring channel runs the length of the ship ... there are inspection hatches in every other compartment. And best of all – the last one opens into the computer section!'

This brought forth grins of delight.

Kerr Avon looked thoughtful. 'If I could have half an hour in there I could open every door in the ship. Knock out the security circuits, blind the scanners.' His pale eyes were wide and unblinking. 'If we hold the computer, then we hold the ship. The crew would be helpless.'

There was a tense silence, broken by Vila's gentle enquiry: 'So when do we move?'

'What's wrong with now?' said Blake.

The words had hardly left his lips when the ship was rocked by a shock wave which sent everyone reeling across the compartment in a tangled confusion of arms and legs. A few managed to grab hold of the bolted-down tables, hanging on as the vessel bucked like a live thing, and there came the grinding, crunching sound of torn metal as chunks of flying debris penetrated the hull.

Those on the Flight Deck had fared no better.

The impact had flung them from their chairs and it was several moments before Captain Leylan and the rest of the Flight personnel were able to regain control of the ship. The situation – as they all realised – was now critical.

'Damage report!' Leylan barked, steadying himself against the Command Desk.

'Port deflector shield buckled,' Raiker reported tersely, scanning the bank of instruments. 'The outer hull has been holed in the stern section.'

'Are the auto-repair circuits coping?'

'They're sealing it,' Raiker confirmed.

'Artix, what have you got?'

'The vision panels are out but I'm getting instrument readings.' The junior officer spared a fleeting glance from the gauges. 'There's an echo from something pretty big on our port, but I can't identify it without a scan.'

Raiker spoke up, his voice thin with urgency. 'Could it be a ship from the battle fleet?'

'Possible.' Artix sounded uncertain. 'But it's a long way out from the centre of the action. It doesn't seem to be under power . . . like it's drifting. My guess is that it's something being pushed along in the shock waves, running parallel to us, but still a long way off.'

'Keep a check on it,' Leylan ordered brusquely. 'And start working on those vision panels –'

He looked up, his face grim and determined as the Flight Deck began to vibrate with the impending impact of another shock wave. They were coming thick and fast now.

'Here we go again,' said Raiker, bracing himself for the shock.

The prisoners in the passenger compartment felt it coming too, but even so they were unprepared for the severity of the tremor which ripped through the ship. Clinging desperately to any fixed object, their faces showed their alarm as the shower of fragments rattled hollowly against the hull. It only needed a single penetration through the inner bulkhead for the air to be sucked out as from a ruptured balloon . . .

'They're getting stronger,' Jenna murmured.

Kerr Avon, releasing his hold on a stanchion as the tremor died away, nodded soberly. 'A couple more like that could shake us to pieces,' he said, voicing everyone's fears.

Blake was preoccupied with briefing some of the other prisoners. He needed their full co-operation if his plan had any chance of success. But as he finished they exchanged uneasy glances; their approval of his scheme was, to say the least, half-hearted.

As they wandered away, Vila observed dryly, 'The chance of freedom hasn't exactly fired them with blood-lust, has it?'

'They've been taking their full rations and getting the maximum dose of suppressants,' Blake pointed out. 'It's knocked all the aggression out of them.'

'Do you think they'll be any use when it comes to it?' Jenna wanted to know.

Blake shook his head doubtfully. 'They'll give us weight of numbers, that's about all.'

'Outside of us, how many have stayed totally off the rations in the last twenty-four hours?' Avon enquired, his pale eyes somewhat disparaging; he didn't seem himself to be in favour of the plan, or perhaps it was Blake's leadership he resented.

Vila ticked them off on his fingers. 'Selman, Klein, Trent.' He pulled a wry face. 'That's about it.'

Avon smiled faintly. 'You've got yourself an army of seven, Blake.' His manner was condescending. 'Still think you can take the ship?'

'You're not thinking of backing out, are you?' Blake's tone was mild, yet his eyes were hard, unyielding.

'I'll do my share,' Avon assured him, meeting his look. 'Don't worry about that.'

'What the hell is that?' Vila muttered, staring at the bulkhead.

A thick gelatine-like substance was oozing from the hairline cracks produced by the vibrations along the inner wall. Jenna touched it lightly, the substance sticking to her fingertips like some kind of heavy congealed glue.

'Sealing gel.' She turned to Blake with the explanation. 'If the outer hull is punctured, this stuff floods into the section and blocks it up. It goes solid in seconds.'

'We were probably holed in that last turbulence,' Avon conjectured.

'While these blast waves keep up we have a better chance,' Blake told them. 'The crew will have their hands full running the ship.'

'Then now is as good a time as any,' Vila agreed.

Blake nodded slowly, considering, then snapped into action. 'Right, give us some cover,' he instructed Vila and Olag Gan. As they went off he turned to Avon. 'We'll be set to move in exactly thirty minutes. That should give you plenty of time.' He glanced up at the wall-mounted lenses set at intervals along the compartment. 'Take out the scanners first. Then get the doors open. We'll reach you as fast as we can.'

'I know what has to be done,' Avon replied tartly.

The covering operation went as smoothly as before. This time Vila demonstrated his hand trick to a fascinated Gan, the pair of them standing near enough to the guard to attract his attention. The prisoners moved across, screening the inspection panel, and under cover of this Blake and Jenna went swiftly about their appointed tasks. It was all over in a matter of moments, and when the knot of prisoners moved away the panel was back in position and Avon had gone.

'How will we know when he's made it?' Jenna breathed.

'The lights on the scanners.' Blake's eyes flicked up to the green light above the nearest scanner which indicated that it was operational. 'When they go out . . . we move.'

5

Artix was fighting against time, struggling desperately to restore the ship's optical sensors. He knelt before the open instrument console, confronted by a maze of solid-state electronics, testing each circuit in turn with a pocket-sized diagnostic device. This is going to take ages, he told himself, trying to keep calm, feeling the sweat gathering between his shoulder-blades.

'How long since the last wave?' Leylan asked Raiker.

The Sub-Commander checked his instruments and did a rapid calculation. 'Seventeen point four minutes.'

'We should be due for another any time now.'

'You ever hit anything like this before?' Raiker asked, his solid, brutal face turning towards the Captain.

'Not this bad.'

'What do you think?'

'If I'm right about the space battle, my guess is a ship with a neutronic motor was hit and blew up.' Lylan ducked his head aside to check on what progress his junior officer was making. 'How are the repairs coming?'

'I haven't located the fault yet,' Artix said, sounding none too happy.

'Are you still getting an echo from that unknown?'

'It's still there, running parallel, but the gap is closing.'

'We're going to need those vision panels,' Raiker said stonily.

'I have another eight circuits to check. If there isn't a fault here, it will be up to the computer operator to locate it...'

'Just get on with it,' Leylan told him, his voice under tight control. Without the vision panels the ship was virtually helpless, a sitting target for whatever that thing was out there, following them as faithfully as a shadow. He wanted to see what it looked like, then maybe he might know what action to take – to either evade or try to deal with it. Though what this old hulk could do in the circumstances amounted to a large fat zero, as Leylan was enough of a realist to admit.

Kerr Avon removed the last of the retaining bolts and eased the inspection panel to one side. This simple manoeuvre was made awkward by the fact that his body was wedged at an angle in the wiring channel. But he had done it, as his first view of the computer room confirmed.

And, what's more, the room was empty!

He silently congratulated himself and slowly lowered the panel to the floor. The computer itself was a free-standing installation in the centre of the room, and even from this distance he recognised it as one of the older-type machines that he'd dealt with years ago. This was going to be child's play, he reckoned, inching his way forward and sliding feet-first through the hatch.

But the next instant he had frozen. Silently and without warning a technician had appeared on the far side of the computer. He had obviously been kneeling down, checking the apparatus, hidden from view. Hardly daring to breathe, Avon retreated back through the hatch and with a swift deft movement replaced the cover, leaving just a tiny slit through which he could observe the technician's movements.

The man hadn't noticed anything, that much was evident,

for he was intently studying a clipboard, no doubt carrying out routine checks.

Avon waited with a growing sense of frustration as the man took his time, wandering round the installation, making minor adjustments. Blake had set a time limit on knocking out the scanners and it was imperative that he get to the computer as quickly as possible. But the fool of a technician was going to take all day with his piddling adjustments!

Wedged in the channel, Avon watched helplessly as the man ticked off another item on the clipboard. He had all the time in the world, it seemed, but for Avon there was precious little of that valuable commodity left.

'He should have made it by now.'

Blake looked anxiously past Jenna's shoulder to the green indicator light on the scanner. He chafed at the delay, counting the passing minutes, knowing that everything depended on Avon reaching the computer room. What the devil could have happened, he wondered morosely.

'You think he's been caught?' Jenna asked, gazing worriedly at Blake.

'I doubt it. There would have been an alarm.' Blake checked his chronometer and spoke in a low urgent tone. 'He must have run into some sort of trouble. I'd better go in after him.'

'I'll go . . . let me do it.'

This from an eager young man standing nearby whose name was Nova. He was certainly keen, Blake thought, but yet he had his doubts.

Vila spoke up. 'He missed the last food distribution. He's reasonably sharp.'

Blake mulled it over and then came to a decision. 'All right,' he agreed. 'Get him in. Start the cover operation.'

Nova smiled gratefully, glad to be given the chance to

help, and the prisoners went into what was now a familiar and practised routine.

For Kerr Avon, time seemed to be passing with the agonising slowness of a placid dream. Still crouched in the constricting space between the outer hull and inner bulkhead, he watched the technician dawdling over his tasks. Would nothing shake him out of his lethargy? Avon asked himself, in a fever of impatience.

One thing would, apparently, for there came the distant though unmistakable shudder of an approaching shock wave, and as the vibration grew in intensity the technician looked round in some alarm. Several loose objects fell from the central console, directly beneath the hatch where Avon was concealed, and the technician came round, stooping to pick them up.

This had to be the moment. Bracing himself, Avon flung the inspection panel aside and exploded into the computer room, dropping on to the unsuspecting man with the full force of his 175 pounds. Stunned, the technician tried to stagger to his feet, and Avon delivered a clean blow to the side of the head that laid him out cold. The man lay sprawled in an untidy heap, his mouth hanging open uselessly.

Then – just as Avon reached the computer – the shock wave hit, and he could do nothing but hang on with dogged determination, feeling the fierce tremor vibrate the fillings in his teeth.

Nova experienced the shock wave even more acutely. He had covered about half the distance along the wiring channel, edging cautiously forward, when the hull resounded with the impact of striking debris. Pressing his hands to his ears, the young man waited grimly for the tremor to subside.

With startling suddenness three small jagged holes appeared in the outer hull and immediately there was the ominous hiss of escaping pressure. Gasping for breath, Nova made a desperate attempt to cover the holes with his hands, and as he did so there was burbling sound that made his head jerk round in mind-numbing horror. From several large nozzles on the inner wall came powerful jets of sealing gel which began to fill up the narrow space. Panic-stricken, Nova tried to claw his way out of the sticky rising tide, but it was futile. Rising up all around, the thick gelatine-like substance completely engulfed him, cutting off his screams of terror in a fast final surge.

On the Flight Deck, Commander Leylan called for a damage report.

'Three hull punctures,' Raiker responded crisply. 'They're already sealed and solid.' He turned to Artix. 'What was the force?'

'Down to seven again. It's reducing.'

Leylan wiped his forehead. 'Not before time. Where's the UFO?'

Artix scanned the instrument panel and there was a rising note of concern in his voice. 'She's damned near up beside us – and still closing.'

'Get those scans fixed!' Leylan shouted at his junior officer. 'Come on – move it!'

The atmosphere in the passenger compartment was just as tense as Blake and the other prisoners watched the indicator lights on the scanners. If neither Avon nor Nova had made the computer room, they were in real trouble, Blake realised.

And then the indicator lights went out.

'He's done it!' Blake said exultantly, and issued curt instructions to the group around him. 'All right . . . take him the moment the door opens,' he said, nodding towards the guard.

But the guard too, it seemed, had noticed something was amiss. A slow stupid frown had crept over his face as he first looked at one of the dead indicator lights and then swivelled to inspect the others.

'He's spotted it,' Jenna said tersely.

Suddenly realising the danger he was in, the guard reached for his communicator, but he wasn't quick enough. Olag Gan sprang forward, snatched it from his fingers, and gripped him firmly, restricting further movement. Before the guard had time to react, Blake, Vila and the other prisoners had closed in all around him.

'The door, Avon.' Blake almost spit the words out. 'Come on . . . *open the door.*'

But Avon was having problems of his own. Having located the control which de-activated the scanners in the passenger compartment, he was now trying desperately to find the master switch that controlled all the doors in the ship. His pale hands skipped across the instrument bank, his mind working in a frenzy as he sought to locate the vital switch.

There it was . . . thank God. Releasing a pent-up breath, his hand closed over the control, but in that same moment a vicious stabbing pain erupted in the base of his skull as the technician chopped down on the back of his neck.

Falling groggily to his knees, Avon had to summon up all his strength as the technician came at him, a murderous glint in his eyes, and the two of them were soon locked in a silent yet deadly struggle.

Blake couldn't wait any longer. 'Bring him here,' he snapped, and Olag Gan half-pushed, half-carried the guard to where Blake stood at the door.

Blake pointed to the glowing blue panel. 'Put your hand there,' he ordered.

The guard glared at them and shook his head stubbornly.

Blake gestured to two of the prisoners. 'Make him,' he said in a low dangerous voice.

They gripped the guard's arm and raised it, forcing his hand towards the panel, but the guard kept it tightly clenched and it was impossible to make him open it, despite their most strenuous efforts.

Olag Gan pushed them aside. He was practically head and shoulders taller than the guard. His face bore a mild, almost dreamy expression as he took hold of the man's wrists in his broad palms and spoke to him very softly.

'It's just your hand we need,' he explained gently. 'If you want to stay attached to it, do as you are told.'

The guard saw the error of his ways. He licked his lips nervously and pressed his hand to the panel. The door slid open.

Led by Blake, who had taken possession of the guard's sidearm, the prisoners surged into the corridor, more hopeful now that they had broken out of their confinement. In the interests of expediency, Gan had hoisted the guard over his shoulder, and carried him along as if he were no more than a rag doll.

Soon they met another closed door, and pushing his way forward, Gan set the guard down on his feet and asked with a charming smile, 'Would you mind?'

This time the guard needed no second bidding.

As the door slid open, Blake issued swift orders. 'Take a few men each and spread out. Try to locate the armoury.' He touched Jenna lightly on the shoulder and indicated that she should stay with him.

The prisoners splintered off in twos and threes, Jenna following Blake at the run. 'Where are we going?' she asked breathlessly, but he was too preoccupied to give her an immediate reply.

In the computer room, Avon leaned weakly against the control panel, steadying himself and getting his wind back. The technician had been a tough customer, requiring all Avon's strength and willpower to overcome him a second time. With trembling fingers he reached forward and threw

6

the master switch that controlled all the doors in the ship.

Raiker was the first to notice the door of the Flight Deck slide back and nobody enter. 'How did that happen?' he muttered, half to himself, but his puzzlement was quickly forgotten as Artix declared:

'The circuits here are all functioning. The fault must be in the computer.'

Leylan jerked his thumb savagely. 'Then get down there.'

Raiker was one stride ahead as they left the Flight Deck and set off down the corridor to the computer room. He faltered at the sight of all the doors standing open.

'Look at the doors – there's something wrong.'

'Maybe the last shake did more damage than we thought,' Artix suggested. 'Looks like the whole system is on the blink.'

'Let's find out,' Raiker grunted, leading the way.

They hurried along the corridor, turned a corner, and both men stopped dead in their tracks, gaping in disbelief.

Blake and the girl were coming towards them!

In the fraction of a second that it took Raiker to react, even while he was fumbling for his sidearm, Blake raised his weapon and aimed an energy bolt which exploded near Raiker's head. The two men dived back round the corner, hefting their sidearms, as Blake and Jenna cautiously advanced. They were caught in the middle of the corridor, with no immediate cover to protect them.

Raiker grinned mercilessly and leapt out, though he was too hasty in his aim and the vivid crackling flare of the energy bolt went wide of its target.

From a doorway halfway along the corridor a head suddenly popped out. It was Kerr Avon. 'Blake!' he yelled, and Jenna gratefully scuttled inside the computer room, Blake backing in after her, covering their retreat.

'Can you close off just this door?' he asked Avon, still watching the corner where Raiker and Artix were concealed.

As Avon found the appropriate control and the door slid

shut, Raiker and Artix came out of hiding and moved purposefully towards the computer room. Raiker took up a position directly facing the door, and holding his sidearm in both hands indicated that the junior officer should activate the blue panel. But when Artix obeyed, the door budged only fractionally and remained closed.

'Damn them!' Raiker cursed, snarling with rage. 'They've got the master switch. Get up to the Flight Deck, tell the old man what's happening.'

Artix sped off and Raiker strode across to a general alarm switch. The loud and continuous blare of a klaxon filled the ship, alerting everyone to be on emergency standby.

In the computer room, Blake stood at Avon's elbow. 'Take out all the control circuits,' he instructed briskly. 'If we can cripple the ship and stay in command of the computer we'll have something to bargain with.'

Avon quickly obeyed, and one by one all the ship's electronic functions died away, the hum and click of electrical relays tailing off to silence and stillness. The ship was lifeless, the lights fading to a dim glow.

Captain Leylan arrived outside the computer room, his face grey and haggard in the murky gloom. 'Are they still in there?' he asked Raiker.

The Sub-Commander nodded, and Leylan snatched up the microphone from a wall communicator and stabbed a button. It only took a moment for Blake's sharp 'Yes?' to issue from the speaker. Leylan squared his shoulders and mustered all the authority he could.

'This is Commander Leylan. If you come out immediately and surrender yourselves you'll be treated leniently. If not, my men will blast their way in and you'll suffer the consequences.'

'Those are your terms?'

'Yes.'

'All right,' Blake snapped. 'Now hear mine. All your weapons are to be handed over to my men. You and your crew will then operate under my orders.' His voice hardened, became completely unyielding. 'You will fly the ship to the nearest habitable planet where we will disembark. While we hold the computer, the ship is helpless. It will stay that way until you agree. One more thing. Any attempt by your men to enter this room and we'll destroy the computer. Totally. We'll all go together. That's all. Let me know when you've decided.'

'Blake . . . wait . . . listen to me,' Leylan said hoarsely. He wiped his mouth with the back of his hand. 'There's a UFO travelling very close to us. We've been running blind for quite a while and for all I know we might be on a collision course. You're putting everybody's life at risk – '

'Then you'd better agree quickly,' Blake retorted, his voice like ice, and the communicator clicked off.

Leylan stared at the wall, then turned to face the others, gesturing helplessly. He was about to speak when there was a sudden burst of firing, very close, and at the far end of the corridor a prisoner lurched into view, clutching his chest. Three armed guards appeared, and on seeing the Captain one of them hurried forward.

'Report,' Leylan ordered.

The guard paused to catch his breath. 'We were very lucky. None of them made it into the armoury. We've got most of them back into their quarters. We're making a thorough search for any stragglers.'

'Good. Casualties?'

'Seven prisoners killed,' the guard reported. 'Some of our men have been injured.'

'All right.' Leylan dismissed him. 'Carry on.'

During this, Raiker had been looking thoughtfully at the door of the computer room. Now a crafty look came into his eyes. 'I can get them out of there,' he said silkily.

'How?'

Raiker stared at him. 'I want a free hand to take whatever action I think necessary. Do I have your permission?'

Leylan hesitated, knowing full well that Raiker's methods for dealing with prisoners were ruthless, devoid of all compassion, but in the circumstances it seemed that he had little choice but to agree. He nodded reluctantly and the Sub-Commander turned on his heel and hurried away.

The tension in the computer room had relaxed slightly: Blake was reasonably confident that now they had taken charge of the ship's vital electronic functions the Commander would have to give in to their demands. As Avon had said, whoever controlled the computer also controlled the ship – and Blake had no intention of relinquishing that control.

He noticed that the technician was starting to come round and alerted Avon to the fact. 'Find something to tie him up,' he ordered, and Avon rummaged in a locker and came up with a length of cable, which he proceeded to use.

'You think they'll buy it?' Jenna asked worriedly, nodding towards the door.

'I'd say we have a reasonable chance,' Blake asserted cheerfully. 'They'll try a few things first, but they don't have long. While we hold this – ' he indicated the central console ' – the ship is in danger. And that puts *them* in danger.'

'Us too,' Jenna added darkly.

But Blake refused to be defeatist. 'Outside of spending the rest of our lives in a prison colony we have nothing to lose. They know that.'

Avon tied a final knot in the cable, binding the technician securely. 'Just assuming they do land us somewhere . . . what then?'

'Somehow or other we get back to Earth.'

'Go back!' Jenna opened her eyes wide and looked at Blake as if he were crazy.

Blake regarded them both, his expression serious and resolute. 'The Administration on Earth is totally corrupt. It goes through to the very highest level. The Justice Department conspired to conceal a mass murder, while other departments just turn a blind eye. There are thousands of other incidents every day where simple human rights are ignored. The people in all the Federated planets are forced to be little more than automatons. Opinion is suppressed, non-conformity is outlawed.' His voice took on a keener cutting edge. 'I want to get the Administration back into the hands of honest men.'

Kerr Avon had listened to this with a faintly mocking expression.

'Very moving,' he said with sardonic disdain. 'Why don't you accept the fact, Blake, that the way things are is the way they'll always be? You won't find me risking my life for the great masses . . . and they won't thank you for it, either. They're happy enough. Fed, clothed, entertained, filled with drugs that keep them sweet and docile.' He shook his head disparagingly. 'Use your intelligence, Blake – just look out for yourself.'

'He's right,' Jenna insisted. 'How can we beat the system? And I'll be quite honest with you, I don't much care about all those downtrodden millions. I just want to be sure *I'm* all right.'

Blake sighed. He was disappointed by these sentiments but he supposed it would have been too naïve to have expected anything different. He spread his hands, conceding their viewpoint. 'I understand. And if we do get out of this . . . well, naturally, what you do is your choice.'

'That's right,' Avon told him. His large pale eyes stared into the middle distance, his mind ticking over with the rapidity of the computers he understood so well. 'As a matter of fact I know exactly what I'd do: adopt a new identity, get myself a job in the Federation banking system . . . then give me three months with their computers and I could quietly lift a hundred million credits and they'd never know where it went. I'd spend the rest of my life on one of those paradise planets –'

The communicator on the central console began to bleep.

Blake strode across and picked up the microphone. 'Yes?'

'Switch on your vision panel.' It was Raiker's voice, his tone flat and menacing. 'Scanner forty-three. There's something you should see . . .'

Avon went to the control panel, pressed a button, and the scanner screen flickered and settled into focus. Blake felt a sinking sensation in the pit of his stomach. The screen showed the passenger compartment ringed by armed guards, in the centre of which the prisoners had been herded into a sullen group, Vila and Gan among them.

Raiker stood to one side, holding the microphone, and as they watched he raised it to his lips. 'Are you on, Blake?'

'We see you.'

'Then keep watching.'

With slow, calm deliberation Raiker took a sidearm from the nearest guard, raised it and pointed the weapon at one of the prisoners. His face betrayed no emotion whatsoever. Sighting along the barrel he pulled the trigger and the man fell to the floor, killed instantaneously.

Raiker turned and said indifferently, 'I'm going to kill one of your friends every thirty seconds starting now. I'll finish when you give yourselves up.'

He held up his wrist and began counting off the seconds.

'Raiker . . . listen to me!' Blake said urgently. 'These men are unarmed prisoners. You have no right to involve them –'

'The talking is over, Blake,' Raiker interjected, still gazing at his chronometer.

'Let me talk to Commander Leylan –'

But Raiker had broken off communication, and on the screen, silently, they saw him raise the weapon. Without even bothering to take particular aim, he fired at point-blank range and another of the prisoners was blasted down in cold blood.

'All right,' Blake said, his face ashen, 'we're giving up. Open the door,' he instructed, and Avon operated the control.

'Stand where you are,' Leylan snapped as the door slid open. He stepped inside, a row of guards at his back. 'Hands on your heads.'

'Raiker's cut off communication,' Blake informed the Captain. 'Tell him we're out – quickly!'

Leylan nodded to Artix, who turned and left the room.

Everyone's attention was fixed on the screen. They saw Raiker, weapon raised, counting off the seconds, and just as he was about to fire Artix came into view and spoke rapidly to him, though they couldn't hear the words. Raiker listened, nodded with evident satisfaction, and fired.

Blake's face went rigid with anger. As the guards bustled him into the corridor he twisted aside and confronted the Captain.

'What happens to us is no longer important, but I demand that this incident is fully reported in your log. Your first officer is guilty of murder.'

'Don't tell me how to run my ship, Blake.' Leylan's tone was crisp but his eyes shifted evasively, as if he too had been shocked by Raiker's callous act. He went on mechanically, 'Everything that happens on this voyage goes on record and is filed with Flight Authority. They'll take any action they feel necessary.'

Blake glared at him, too angry for words, and turned abruptly to face Raiker and Artix as they came along the corridor.

Raiker was triumphant, his whole manner that of the arrogant strutting bully. 'You had a perfect chance, Blake,' he sneered. 'If you'd held out you could have won. You just didn't have the guts to watch the others die.'

Blake went for him, all the hatred spilling out, unable to contain it, and Raiker swung the butt of his sidearm and caught Blake a stunning blow on the side of the jaw. He staggered back, semi-conscious, the guards hauling roughly at his shoulders.

'Take them back,' Raiker commanded. 'Place them in close confinement.'

As they were dragged away, Leylan tried to regain some of his lost authority. 'Artix, get a repair squad in there. I want that computer on full function in twenty minutes.' He started back for the Flight Deck, Raiker at his side. They had walked a little way before Leylan ventured to say quietly, 'You went too far, Raiker. There'll have to be an enquiry.'

The Sub-Commander was in complete agreement. 'Naturally, sir. And I'm sure you will confirm that I was acting with your full authority.' He smiled with easy, smug assurance, noting Leylan's nervous, almost apprehensive manner, and added softly, 'There were other officers present who heard you give me permission to do what was necessary.'

The message was plain enough; but Leylan still retained some professional pride, and Raiker's smile slipped when the Commander said brusquely:

'Everything that was said or done by everybody – and that includes me – will be in my report. *Every*thing.'

Blake struggled through a mist of pain and surfaced to find himself pinned in the launch seat, firmly secured by the curved metal bands. He looked hazily around him, wincing as the deep throbbing ache in his jaw reminded him that Raiker had got the upper hand during their last encounter. A battle, he told himself grimly, but not the war.

'How is it?' Jenna enquired from a nearby seat. She and Kerr Avon were also in close confinement.

'It hurts,' Blake replied succinctly.

Avon was in an ugly mood. 'I was stupid to let you lead me into this mess. I went against my instincts. I knew I shouldn't have become involved.'

'What do you think they'll do to us?' Jenna asked, straining to look at Blake.

'Nothing we'll enjoy.'

'You know, for a while there I really thought we were going to make it.' Jenna's face was sad, resigned. 'I didn't see how we could fail . . .'

'It was my mistake,' Blake admitted, easing himself against the metal bands. 'We'll do better next time.'

'Next time!' Avon burst out incredulously.

'Don't you ever give up?' Jenna demanded, studying him intently.

Blake shook his head obstinately, his eyes staring straight ahead. 'There's too much to be done.'

6

Commander Leylan looked about him with a growing sense of confidence as one by one the ship's electronic systems came back to life; he felt more in control of the situation as he saw the banks of instrumentation light up and start to resume their functions. Familiar and reassuring – and with the ship on full operational status once again he permitted himself a tiny smile of relief. He glanced up from the Command Desk as Artix came on to the Flight Deck and settled in his seat.

'We have full response on all systems,' the Flight Operator advised him. 'They're phasing them in now.'

'Do we have scan yet?'

'No, sir.'

'Then get an instrument reading on the UFO,' Leylan rapped.

Artix checked a sequence of dials and almost leapt out of his chair.

'It's right alongside us!'

Raiker glanced across to confirm the reading. 'If this is accurate we're almost touching,' he told Leylan with a worried frown.

A blue light winked on.

'That's it!' Artix yelped excitedly. 'We've got the scan back.' He began feverishly to operate the controls, and in a few moments the large scanner screen swam with colours and distorted images before settling down into sharp brilliant focus.

The three men gazed at the screen, awestruck. Nobody spoke. The silence seemed to hum in their ears, all of them lost for words, until finally Raiker ventured to say in a small lost voice:

'She's fantastic . . . '

'Look at her size,' Leylan mouthed, dumbfounded.

'Where's she from?' Artix whispered.

Leylan shook his head in bewilderment. 'I've never seen anything like her before in my life. There's no planet in the known galaxies that could build a ship like that . . . '

The main body of the ship was headed by a brilliant green power unit that seemed to throb and glow as they watched. Three arms branched out from the central core, forming a tripod effect, and each arm was tipped with lethal weaponry of a sophistication that none of them and ever witnessed before.

Leylan shook himself, as if coming out of a trance. 'She looks to me like she's drifting, Mister Raiker. Take over and fly us on manual. Keep the same distance between us.'

'Yes, sir.' The Sub-Commander settled in position in front of the flight controls and concentrated on keeping the *London* on a steady even course.

'Mister Artix, try and make contact. Sound and vision.'

Artix pulled the microphone towards him and flicked the control to multi-channel communication. 'This is Civil Administration ship *London* out of Earth for Cygnus Alpha. We are holding a position on your port bow. Please identify yourself.'

They waited tensely, but the only response was a faint crackle of static from the speaker.

'Try again,' Leylan ordered. 'Put it through the translator unit. Run the message in every known language.'

'You want my guess?' Raiker offered, glancing towards

the Commander. 'She was involved in that space battle we picked up. Probably got caught in the big blast and her crew were either killed or got out in the life-rockets.'

Leylan studied the screen. 'Possible,' he conceded, 'But she doesn't show any sign of damage.'

'No signs of life either,' Raiker remarked.

The two men looked at one another, the same thought in both their minds.

'If she's been abandoned . . .' Leylan muttered casually.

'We could put on a boarding party.' Raiker's eyes lit up greedily. 'You know what that ship would be worth in prize money if we could get her to a Federation planet? Millions of credits. Millions!'

'Leave a skeleton crew on her . . . ' Leylan mused. 'We could do it.'

'It's got to be worth a try,' urged Raiker.

The Commander came to a decision. 'We'll give it a go.' He leaned forward, snapped down a switch and spoke into the communicator:

'Section Four! Stand by to run out a transfer tube from starboard lock six. Wallace and Teague, kit out with survival units. I'll be with you in a minute.' He stood up and turned to Raiker. 'Take us as close as you can and then hold firm.'

The Sub-Commander nodded, his concentration centred on the delicate manoeuvre of bringing the *London* to within boarding range of the strange new craft. His fingers trembled slightly at the thought of what exotic valuables she might contain; indeed, he was more concerned with her monetary value than with any passing thought as to where she had suddenly and mysteriously appeared from.

Poised in space, the brilliant starlight reflecting a soft lambent sheen from the smooth graceful lines of her massive hull, the alien spacecraft dwarfed the *London* as an ocean

93

liner would overshadow a diminutive tub bringing her into port.

As the two vessels, seemingly motionless, rode together less than thirty metres apart, a square hatch on the *London*'s starboard quarter slid open and a flexible, concertina-like tube began slowly to extend, wavering like a blind searching snout as it spanned the vacuum between them.

Standing outside the airlock, Leylan watched on the scanner as the transfer tube neared the spacecraft's hull, then jerked forward with a final sudden surge as the electromagnetic clamps drew it into position.

'Locked on, sir,' the crewman confirmed, glancing up from the control panel.

Leylan nodded brusquely and gestured to Wallace and Teague, who were already fully equipped with lightweight breathing apparatus and an assortment of scientific instruments clipped to their belts. And as per standard regulations, they also carried sidearms.

'Keep your communicators open at all times,' Leylan instructed the two men. 'I want a full report on conditions inside that ship. If there's anything living over there, you'll try to make peaceful contact. Weapons are not to be used unless you have definite evidence of hostility. Understood?'

Wallace and Teague nodded behind their tinted faceplates and stepped up to the inner hatch.

'Open airlock,' Leylan called, and the hatch slid back. The two men advanced into the small chamber, the hatch closed, and a few moments later came the dull thud of the outer door sliding open.

Leylan folded his arms, gnawing his lower lip, and raised his head alertly as the sound of heavy breathing issued from the speaker.

'Starting along the transfer tube now, sir.' Teague's voice.

More muffled breathing. Leylan caught the eye of the crewman at the control panel, whose tense expression mirrored his own. Then:

'We're against the hull. There's a hatch entrance.' A slight pause. 'I'm about to operate the anti-lock device.'

Teague's breathing had steadied somewhat. After a moment he reported, 'No response on circuit one. I'll try the others . . . no response on circuit two. No response on circuit three. No response on circuit . . .'

Leylan stared at the speaker grille, his eyes clouded with anxiety.

'Wait!' Teague's excited voice. 'Yes . . . it's opening!'

Leylan let go a breath. He suddenly became aware that his upper arms were tingling from the pressure of his curled fingers.

'Powerful light source emanating from the interior . . . moving inside now.'

Leylan beckoned to a crewman, his voice gruff with urgency. 'You! Get kitted up. Then stand by to give back-up if it's needed.'

'We're in a sort of cylinder,' Teague was saying. 'Type of airlock, I think.' His voice heightened with panic. 'It's turning!'

The speaker went silent and Leylan yelled, 'Report! Report!'

There was a further silence, and then to Leylan's relief Teague's voice continued, 'It's fantastic . . . I can't believe it . . .'

'What is it?' Leylan barked. 'What's happening?'

'It's all right, we've come out into what must be a flight deck.' Teague's voice faltered, became almost dreamlike. 'But it's like nothing I've ever seen . . .'

'Describe it later. Give me an instrument reading.'

'Pressure normal. Minimal radiation. Breathable oxygen atmosphere.'

'Good. Now is there anybody on board?'

'Not that we've seen, but I – I'm sorry – what was that? I didn't hear . . .'

'I said nothing.'

'Somebody spoke. I heard a voice and it – '

A deafening burst of static erupted from the speaker. It ceased abruptly and there was nothing. Absolute silence.

'Teague, report at once! *Teague!*' Leylan looked wildly around. 'Where the hell is that back-up man? They could be in trouble.'

The crewman, Krell, appeared, buckling on his gear.

'Get across there as fast as you can.' Leylan hustled him towards the airlock; immediately he was inside he strode to the wall communicator and punched a button, linking him with the Flight Deck. 'Raiker, get down here right away. Let Artix take over the ship.'

By the time the Sub-Commander had arrived Krell had made his way along the transfer tube. Standing tensely at Leylan's side, Raiker listened to the crewman's voice over the speaker.

'I'm in the airlock and it's turning.' There was a long pause. 'I'm inside. The design is strange to me. All the flight control positions are empty.'

'All right,' Leylan interrupted. 'Now don't move for a moment. Just look round, tell me what you see.'

Krell's voice steadied, as if carefully gathering his thoughts together. 'There's an incredible complex of instrumentation, none of it activated. There's a sort of . . . globe . . . seems to be lit from inside. It's suspended by – wait a moment, I heard something.'

'What is it?'

'It's whispering,' said Krell in a strange lost voice. 'Yes . . . yes, I hear you,' he went on vacantly. 'David? What are you doing – ' Then, in a terrifying shriek that was pain and anger combined, 'What are they doing to you? No! No! *No!*'

The speaker flared up once again in a crackling burst of static, drowning everything; it was followed by a deadening hush.

'Krell, answer me!' Leylan shouted. 'Krell!' He glanced at Raiker, his eyes wide with fear, then gripped the microphone firmly. 'Listen to me. If I have no signal from you in three minutes I'm hauling in the transfer tube and breaking contact.'

'Wait!' Raiker snarled, grabbing his arm. 'We can't give up that easily. It's too valuable – that ship is worth a fortune.'

'Chances are I've already lost three men,' Leylan told him stolidly. 'I'm not risking any more lives.'

'But we've got to find out how, why.'

'I won't put any more of my crew in danger,' Leylan insisted.

'Then use prisoners.' Raiker's eyes were bright, alive with the idea. 'They've got nothing to lose. Use Blake and the other two.' And when Leylan didn't immediately object, 'Let them take the risks . . . why not?'

The Commander mulled the scheme over. 'They just might learn something,' he agreed slowly.

'Right! They could feed back enough information so that we can put on a proper boarding party. If they don't make it – ' he shrugged dismissively ' – well then at least we've tried.'

He waited, fretting, and Leylan said finally, 'Get them equipped and bring them down here.'

'I hope Mister Raiker made it clear that you can refuse to undertake this job.'

Commander Leylan stood facing the three prisoners, who had already been issued with lightweight breathing apparatus, looking intently at each of them in turn. He was loath to risk more lives, but as Raiker had pointed out, prisoners on their way to the Penal Colony had little to lose . . . and he desperately wanted to know what had happened to his crewmen in that strange alien spacecraft.

Blake finished buckling on his equipment. 'He also made it clear that there's a mandatory death sentence for mutiny.'

He added with a trace of sarcasm, 'He didn't leave too many choices.'

'Do this and I give you my word I'll have that sentence quashed,' Leylan promised.

Jenna held her head high, staring at him coldly. 'What is it we have to do?'

'Find out what's happened to my men and if possible make it safe for a boarding party to go across.'

'All right,' Blake agreed. 'What about you two?' he asked Jenna and Avon.

Jenna raised one eyebrow sardonically. 'Why not?'

Avon seemed more reluctant, but then he too nodded.

'Good,' Leylan said briskly. 'I can't give you much to go on, just that the other men appeared to hear voices. Then we lost contact.'

Blake frowned. 'Nothing else?'

'Nothing significant.'

Raiker was holding three belts containing loaded side-arms and Blake pointed to them. 'Do we get weapons?'

'I'll toss them into the airlock,' Raiker grinned nastily. 'Once you're inside.'

'Not taking any chances, are you?' Blake stepped forward, squaring his shoulders. 'All right, we're ready. Open the lock.'

The hatch slid back and a spitting, clawing madman leapt out at them.

With a fearsome strangled cry he hurled himself straight at Leylan and took him about the throat, the two of them crashing to the floor, Krell babbling and shrieking like something whose mind has snapped, gone forever beyond the point of no return.

The sudden shock of his appearance stunned everyone, but in the next moment two crewmen jumped forward and hauled him off Leylan, who rose shakily to his feet, his face white and strained.

Krell had subsided into a mindless, gibbering wreck, his

eyes staring aimlessly into space, his jaw working uselessly. Saliva dribbled down his chin.

'Get him out of here,' Leylan ground out, finding his voice.

'What did that to him?' Jenna asked, looking round with horrified fascination.

Avon clicked his tongue. 'That is what we're supposed to find out,' he remarked caustically. 'Compared to that, execution has a certain appeal.'

'Come on.' Blake moved forward into the airlock. 'Let's get started.'

His two companions joined him and all three waited tensely as the airlock was activated. Stepping carefully from the outer hatch they found themselves in a swaying translucent tube, dimly illuminated on all sides by the surrounding panorama of hard brilliant stars. It was eerily silent, as if they were being observed by a million eyes from every corner of the Universe; advancing cautiously, they slowly approached the oval hatchway, which blazed with a powerful dazzling glow.

The body of a crewman – it was Wallace – lay inside, his legs drawn up into a tight foetal position. His expression was closed and blank behind the tinted faceplate.

The chamber inside the hatchway was smooth and circular, like the interior of a vertical cylinder, and made of a curious non-metallic material that was warm to the touch. As soon as they entered, the chamber began to turn – apparently of its own accord – sealing off the outer door, and Blake got the distinct impression that the cylinder was revolving upwards in a long gentle spiral, though there was little sensation of movement.

They turned with it, so that when it had completed half a revolution they were facing into the ship, and as the large oval door locked into position they were confronted with a sight which, quite literally, took their breath away ...

None of them, least of all Blake, ever forgot their first view of the magnificent Flight Deck of the deep space cruiser they were to come to know as the *Liberator*.

Positioned round a central vertical column were five seats, rather like bicycle saddles with high backs and head-rests, where the operatives could sit with their concentration trained on the pilot. At each seat was a small computer terminal and unit, gleaming softly in the glowing light.

Jenna was the first to move forward, gazing round as if in some electronic wonderland that before now had been confined to her dreams. Indeed, it seemed like a dream, the perfect functional symmetry of its design reminding her of a piece of superb modern architecture.

'It's beautiful,' she breathed, truly in awe. 'A ship like this could go anywhere in the Universe.'

Avon was just as mesmerised. 'Look at that instrument-ation,' he murmured, with the heightened appreciation of the connoisseur. 'It's twenty or thirty generations ahead of the most advanced stuff we've got.'

He swivelled round and then stiffened as his eye fell on something lying partly concealed by one of the modules. It was Teague, his body wound tightly in the same position as the other crewman.

'What's that?' Jenna enquired softly, lifting her head at a subdued yet persistent humming sound. It seemed to be coming from above their heads.

'I don't know,' Blake answered, perplexed, and then all three of them saw it, floating high up near the curved ceiling . . . a perfectly spherical globe which burned with a soft inner radiance. It was suspended in the air, drifting very slowly, and as they watched, fascinated, it began to pulse with a fierce radiant glow.

Jenna felt her senses start to slide. It wasn't unpleasant at first, this vague sliding world, until the voice began to hiss in her ear:

' . . . help me, Jenna, help me . . . they're hurting me, Jenna, help me . . . please help me, Jenna . . . '

And then it wasn't pleasant at all, it was grotesque and

frightening as the images entered her mind and she was powerless to resist them. They drew her forward, beckoning her into their world, and she wanted to stop, to go back, to fight them, but she was helpless against their gentle insistent call.

Avon too had entered his own private nightmare – his eyes fixed unblinkingly on the radiant sphere, hearing another voice that begged and pleaded with him:

' . . . don't leave me, please . . . I need you . . . please don't leave me . . . '

The low persistent hum had gradually risen so that it now filled the air with a high-pitched keening whine that seemed to beat inside their heads. The sphere was glowing with an intense brightness, and Blake too found himself drawn irresistibly towards it. He pressed his hands over his ears in an attempt to overcome its malevolent influence, but deep within his mind a voice was calling to him, whispering the same words over and over again:

' . . . my son, don't let them take me . . . please help me, help me . . . please, my son . . . '

He fought against it, this voice that was at once so gently familiar and yet so evil. Clenching his fists, he drove his nails into the palms of his hands, the pain breaking through the pervasive illusion and jerking him back to reality –

And was horrified to see Jenna and Avon advancing slowly towards the sphere, arms outstretched, their eyes glazed and lost in visions.

Gathering every ounce of mental and physical strength he possessed, Blake lunged forward, crying out, 'Keep back! Jenna – Avon – No! NO!'

They continued to move towards the pulsing brightness, paying him no heed, and Blake threw himself at Jenna, dragging her back. He turned swiftly and tried to grab Avon by the shoulder; but with a single backward sweep of his arm, Avon sent him sprawling. Climbing grimly to his feet, Blake went after him again, this time making no mistake as he delivered a blow to Avon's jaw which knocked him to the floor.

Yet Jenna was still under the influence of the radiant globe, approaching as in a trance with her arms raised, her quivering fingertips seeking to touch it. The glow seemed to enfold her.

With frantic haste, Blake wrenched his sidearm from its holster and aimed directly at the pulsing light. There was a blinding flare as the sphere disintegrated – an instant of dazzling brightness which was pierced by Jenna's scream as she slumped to the floor. Blake ran to her and cradled her in his arms.

'What was it?' she murmured distantly, trying to focus on his face.

'I don't know . . . some sort of hallucinatory device.'

'I saw my mother. She was so real. Then terrible things, like a nightmare.' Jenna regarded him earnestly. 'But it was my mother.'

'No,' said Blake, shaking his head. 'That thing was able to take an image out of your mind – a memory – and project it back at you as though it were real.'

Avon rose groggily to his feet, rubbing his jaw. 'I saw my brother. That thing used him like some sort of bait.' His expression contorted. 'I had to go closer.'

'And if you had it would have killed you.'

'How did you break out?' Jenna frowned.

'I don't know,' Blake confessed frankly. 'I saw the images, heard the voices, but somehow I hung on to the fact it wasn't real. Remember, there have been whole areas of my memory that were erased . . . maybe that's what saved me.'

Avon looked around the Flight Deck, as if searching for other auto-hypnotic devices. 'Well, however it works, it's a near-perfect protection system,' he declared with grudging admiration.

Blake's communicator buzzed and he thumbed the receiver button.

'Blake, are you receiving me?' asked Commander Leylan urgently. 'Are you all right?'

'Yes, we're safe,' Blake answered, looking at the other two. And before Leylan could respond with further instructions, 'Still checking. Out.'

Avon had gone across to the main control desk and was inspecting the complex instrument panel. He called Blake over. 'This accounts for what happened to the crew,' he informed him, motioning to a square red tab inside a transparent rectangular box arrangement. The hinged lid was open.

'What is it?'

'Life rocket launch control. See – it's been operated.'

'Then they abandoned,' Blake surmised.

'I wonder why?' Jenna mused, idly trailing her fingers over a series of oval buttons. Instantly a bank of green indicator lights flashed on. 'The whole ship looks like it's in operational condition.'

Blake was studying the five control positions grouped round the main command module. 'Could she fly under her own power?' he enquired nonchalantly.

'I can't see why not.'

'Could you pilot her?'

Jenna laughed. 'A ship like this?' She shook her head ruefully. 'Not a chance. Give me a couple of hours checking the systems and I might just be able to make the lights come on . . . but that's about all.'

Blake said, 'You've got a couple of minutes, no more.'

The other two stared at him, their mouths hanging open.

'We're going to take her.' He looked at each of them in turn, his face deadly serious, then set off for the oval door.

Avon found his voice. 'Where are you going?'

Blake didn't break his stride. 'To close the entry hatch before they decide to land a full boarding crew.'

He entered the circular chamber and as it turned through

180 degrees, he clipped his faceplate into position. A sixth sense warned him that they had precious little time if they were going to succeed in sneaking the ship away from under the noses of Leylan and Raiker. He had seen the greed in their faces and knew without any doubt that any promises they might have made were just so much empty air.

The airlock revolved and came into line with the open hatchway. Blake stepped forward, began to search for the control that would close it – and saw Raiker.

He was about halfway along the transfer tube, one hand outstretched to steady himself, the other gripping his sidearm. Blake fumbled for his own weapon, only to find the holster empty. Cursing himself, he remembered it was lying on the floor of the Flight Deck where he had dropped it when rushing to help Jenna.

Raiker had seen him too, and Blake knew that his only chance now was to close the hatch. But even as he sought to locate the control Raiker braced himself in the swaying tube and fired. There was the gritty crunch of an energy bolt exploding near Blake's head and he ducked back into cover.

Where was that damn control?

Raiker was nearer now, his eyes hard and menacing behind the faceplate. Again he fired and Blake felt a searing pain in his left shoulder. The impact spun him and flung him backwards so that he lay on his side in the open hatchway, exposed and helpless, an unmissable target. And still Raiker came on, only metres away.

With cold deliberation he raised his sidearm, his lips parting in a snarl of triumph, and pointed it unerringly at Blake's supine figure. His finger curled on the trigger, and in that same instant the end of the transfer tube became detached from the hull as the *Liberator*, under Jenna's tentative guiding hand, curved away on a new flight trajectory.

Raiker had a moment's grace before the sub-zero vacuum sucked the air out of the tube, him with it, and his mouth gaped in a ghastly silent scream as he floated away, spreadeagled against the starry backdrop, until he was no more than an insignificant motionless speck in the infinite void of deep space.

'We're on our way!' Jenna said exultantly, looking up with shining eyes as Blake came on to the Flight Deck.

'You're hurt,' Avon frowned, noticing Blake's wounded shoulder.

'I'll take care of it when we've set a course.'

'All right, just name it,' Jenna said confidently, settling at the controls with a child's eager anticipation. 'We're free. We've got a ship. We can go anywhere we want!'

Blake sank down into one of the six deeply-padded control positions. 'We're going to follow the *London* to Cygnus Alpha.' His voice was quiet, unemotional, yet filled with absolute resolve. 'We're going to free the rest of the prisoners. And then, with a full crew, we're going to start fighting back!'

7

It was a bleak and desolate place, a planet of barren rock and stunted vegetation, wreathed in sulphurous mist. This, the furthermost frontier of manned exploration, was the perfect location on which to site a penal colony, many parsecs distant from the centre of galactic civilisation. Escape was impossible, the inmates doomed to live the rest of their lives in primitive squalor on a lost world, forgotten and abandoned in outer darkness.

Crouched over a small fire, the carcase of rodent roasting smokily on a sharpened stick, two hooded figures gazed with dulled eyes into the flickering flames. Crude sackcloth robes enveloped them like shrouds; their faces were hidden in the deep shadow cast by the hooded cowls.

Grunting, the one nearest the fire reached out a scrawny arm and removed the sizzling carcase from the flame and laid it on a flat rock. From his wide sleeve he removed a knife and with its broad iron blade slashed downwards, a swift savage stroke, splitting the carcase in two. Taking the larger portion, he began to eat, tearing at the flesh and sucking the hot juices from his fingers. His companion took the remaining portion, and for a time the only sounds in the clearing were the crackling flames and the gnawing and crunching of tiny animal bones.

Then, faintly, from high above, another sound.

The two shrouded figures became still; rising slowly, they stared upwards into the night sky, listening intently as the sound grew louder until it was descernible as the roar of a rocket engine. And now they could see it, the fiery glow descending towards the planet.

The taller figure made a guttural noise and the hooded cowl fell back a little to reveal his face. It was gaunt, deeply lined, framed by wild hair, a cruel and violent face in which the eyes brooded like cold black pebbles.

'A Federation ship,' Laran gloated, his teeth bared in a soulless grin. 'Bringing in prisoners.'

His companion turned to him . . . and in the flickering firelight it was a face of evil, the lips twisted in a rapacious snarl, yet even so with a fascinating, hypnotic beauty.

'New souls for the faith,' said Kara in a throaty whisper, her eyes alight with sly rapture. She tore the last of the meat from the bone, throwing it into the fire where it spat and sizzled. 'We must go to Him and tell Him there is new bounty come from the outer darkness . . .'

Together they watched as the glowing orb of light slowly descended towards the desolate wasteland of Cygnus Alpha.

Commander Leylan stood pensively before the scanner screen watching the planet loom gradually larger, much of its surface masked by dense layers of swirling grey mist. He shivered involuntarily; even to visit such a hell-hole of a world for a few short hours filled him with a sense of uneasy foreboding. It was the place of the damned, lost souls crying in the wilderness.

His morbid reverie was interrupted by his junior officer, who came to stand at his elbow. For Artix, landing on one of the planets of the outer systems was still a thrilling experience.

'How long before we put in?' he asked, a slight catch in his voice.

'About fourteen STUs,' Leylan answered bleakly. He adjusted a control dial and the planet's misty outline sharpened into focus, some of its topographical features becoming clearly visible. 'Are the prisoners quiet?'

'We're dosing the air supply with suppressant vapour. They're under constant scan. I've put on double guards and the crew is armed.'

Leylan smiled wanly and turned away. 'All a bit late in the day now,' he remarked, leaning over the Command Desk and scribbling a rapid note. He handed it to Artix. 'I want you to send this. Beam it to the nearest Federation base and have them relay it to Earth.'

Artix glanced at the note and looked up, frowning. 'This will go against us on our records, I suppose –'

'We won't get medals,' said Leylan flatly. 'Send it.'

Artix moved to the communications console and spoke crisply into the microphone. 'This is Civil Administration ship *London* in transit from Earth to Cygnus Alpha, transporting prisoners to the Penal Colony. We have sustained crew casualties during an attempted mutiny by prisoners. Five dead, including Sub-Commander Raiker. Three prisoners escaped in a spacecraft of unknown origin. Prisoners Blake, Stannis and Avon. The *London* is again under authorised control and proceeding to destination. Message ends. Retransmit to Earth on priority circuit. Confirm.'

He waited, and after a brief interval an indicator light winked on the panel. 'We have confirmation.'

Leylan was once again studying the screen. He altered the setting and the image changed to a starscape, many of the constellations of a strange configuration, way beyond the frontiers of the colonised system. His expression was morose, the set of his shoulders bowed under the weight and responsibility of duty.

'Will they send ships after Blake?' Artix enquired, standing beside him.

'They have to.'

'There are a lot of places out there to hide.'

'No.' Leylan spoke with quiet emphasis. 'Hiding is not Blake's style. I've read his record. He'll hit back. And unless they get him quickly he'll keep on hitting back ...'

Artix glanced sideways at the Commander's stern profile, suddenly sensing that perhaps their troubles were not yet over, and then returned his gaze to the spread of stars against the blue-blackness of space.

Somewhere out there, that same starlight glinted on the huge impressive bulk of the space cruiser *Liberator* as she moved at low torque through the stellar night. Myriad highlights of topaz and magenta sparkled on the graceful curve of her prow: a dazzling ship of state with all the majesty and power that an advanced technological civilisation could bestow.

And at the controls, Jenna Stannis, flying her with a none-too-easy hand.

Only now were the three of them beginning to realise what a marvellous prize they had won. The Flight Deck itself was a treasure-house of sophisticated instrumentation, daunting in the scale and variety of its multifarious control systems. So far they could only guess at the function of most of them, and it would be some time before they felt themselves to be in complete confident command of the *Liberator*'s complex electronic network.

Exploring a bank of lockers built flush into the bulkhead behind the central command position, Blake came upon a rack of handguns fitted into holstered belts. They were of a design he'd never seen before, a coiled cable leading from the butt to what appeared to be a power unit built into the belt. Some kind of concentrated energy source, Blake surmised. He called Avon across and together they examined them.

'I wonder how it works?' Blake mused aloud, hefting the beautifully engineered weapon and squinting along the burnished barrel.

'Careful with that,' Avon cautioned him nervously. 'You can play around when we touch down somewhere.'

Blake grinned at him and strapped on the belt. 'Whatever they do, they give a nice sense of protection.'

'I'd say that clinches it.' Avon balanced the handgun in his palm. 'Whatever race built and crewed this ship were humanoid.' He held the weapon up. 'The butt of this is shaped for a hand like ours.' Strapping on the belt, he added, 'And they also had waists,' struggling a little to fasten the buckle.

'But slimmer than yours,' Blake commented with a wry smile. 'You're right though – the seating, the controls, they were built by a species like us.'

He took one of the belts across to Jenna and told her to put it on. She carefully checked the controls first, then gingerly let go.

'How does she handle?'

'Beautifully,' Jenna smiled, in love with the entire ship. 'I'm getting the hang now. From what I've seen so far there's nothing like her in the Federation.' Jenna's eyes shone. 'She's centuries ahead –'

'Same with all this,' declared Avon enthusiastically, spreading his arms wide. 'It's not just advanced on what we know – it's a whole different technology!'

Jenna had settled herself at the flight control module. She indicated the rows of switches and buttons grouped in sequences of colours. 'There are a whole lot of controls I haven't dared touch yet,' she admitted.

'Try one,' Blake invited.

'And if it turns out to be Self-Destruct?'

'Then who'll be around to blame you?' Blake asked, his eyes amused as he watched her slim hand hovering over the complex array.

'I'd like to find Autoflight,' Jenna murmured, concentrating hard. 'There must be one . . .'

'Go ahead – try.'

As if selecting a chocolate from a box, Jenna suddenly decided on a button that appealed to her and pressed it decisively. None of them was prepared for the massive power surge as the ship suddenly accelerated, throwing Blake and Avon off balance and pressing Jenna deeply into the padded chair. There was an accompanying howl from the engines as speed built up, and all of them felt their vision fading under the vastly increased g forces. With an effort, Jenna reached forward and managed to deactivate the acceleration control, falling back with a sigh when the ship steadied and resumed normal flight.

'No, I don't think that's the one,' Blake muttered, straightfaced, recovering his stance.

'Power thrust of some kind,' Jenna said. 'I was blacking out.'

'I got that too.

'That wasn't just g force blackout,' Avon decided. 'You know what I think? We were going through light barriers.'

Blake shook his head in wonderment. 'That could rock a few cherished theories. Try something else.'

Jenna shrugged and stabbed at another button. 'Hold on, this could be emergency eject.'

But nothing happened. Or seemed to happen.

Until from nowhere a soft expressionless voice with a slightly grating texture began to chant a series of phrases:

Trell zen. Ravan goll havall zen regin. Zen. Zen.

'There's somebody else on the ship!' Jenna said, alarmed.

'No, it's computer-speak,' Avon informed them, striding across to an oval grille above which a pattern of lights had begun to flash. 'See, it's mechanical.'

'Do you recognise the language?' Blake enquired.

Avon shook his head, studying what appeared to be a random sequence of winking lights on the panel. There was a rapid yet subdued chatter of relays and the lights adopted a new configuration, which remained constant. From the grille issued the same gentle, though slightly mechanical, voice:

'The translator units have identified your language. The auto-navigation computers have re-circuited to accept your speech commands. State speed and course.'

The three of them looked at each other, bemused and not a little bewildered.

Jenna regarded Blake impishly. 'Go ahead – tell it what to do.'

Blake cleared his throat and spoke up. 'I want a course to the planet Cygnus Alpha. Standard cruising speed.'

There was a moment's delay while the pattern of lights changed sequence.

'Course and speed confirmed.'

Jenna suddenly let go of the controls. 'It's flying itself.'

'I'll tell you something.' Avon folded his arms and looked slowly round the Flight Deck. 'I'm very impressed.'

'What was the word it kept repeating? Zen?' Jenna asked.

'I just wonder what else Zen is capable of,' Avon muttered.

'We'll find out in good time,' Blake promised. 'Anyway, now we're on our way, let's take a look round the rest of the ship. Going by what we've seen so far I'd say we've got ourselves a pretty impressive piece of equipment.'

He nodded thoughtfully, leading the way towards an inner port at the rear of the Flight Deck, and paused there with the others while they turned and surveyed their new domain in silent admiration. The ship's full complement was six, and so far there were only three of them. But at least it was a start.

The Flight Controller, his young face with its embryo beard fixed in total concentration, was counting in decreasing order from the gauge on the instrument panel in front of him.

' . . . seventeen . . . sixteen . . . fifteen . . . '

'Landing beam aligned and locked in,' Leylan intoned.

' . . . fourteen . . . thirteen . . . twelve . . . '

'Cut main anti-gravs.'

Artix hit a bank of throttle levers and the pulsing roar of the engines faded to a low murmuring growl.

'Anti-gravs off,' Artix confirmed.

'Entering silo. We have ground contact. All off.'

Leylan flicked a row of switches and both men relaxed as the sound died away to complete silence. The *London* had made landfall on Cygnus Alpha.

The Commander allowed himself only a moment before sliding out from behind the control position. He rapped out briskly, 'Disembark the prisoners, Mister Artix. Full security until they're in the reception block. I'll programme the computers for the return trip. We blast off in ten minutes.'

Artix raised his eyebrows in surprise. 'What's the hurry? We've been in space for eight months. I'd like to feel some ground under my feet – '

'You wouldn't if you knew what this place was like,' Leylan shot back dourly. He moved across to the navigational computer console. 'Now get the prisoners off and let's get out of here.'

Artix made a slight shrugging motion and headed for the exit. 'Yes sir,' he said under his breath, wondering if Cygnus Alpha could really be as bad as all that.

'Well, what do you think?'

Following a maze of corridors, Blake and Avon had eventually found themselves in a large circular chamber which contained a curious arrangement of curved open-sided cubicles, a large control panel and a rack of what appeared to be elaborately-designed metal bracelets. A clockface marked off in coloured segments was mounted prominently on one wall. The purpose of the chamber wasn't immediately clear, which was what had prompted Blake's question.

Avon turned from his examination of the cubicles and looked towards the control panel. 'It's some sort of transmission device. Probably breaks down the molecular structure of matter and transmits it through space as particles of energy.'

'You think it would work on living matter? Flesh and blood?'

Avon pursed his lips, considering. 'If it did we could get ourselves teleported down to the surface of the planet without ever having to land the ship.' He grinned ruefully and gave Blake a look. 'But just in case I'm wrong I'm not going to be the first to try it.'

Blake had taken one of the bracelets from the rack and was inspecting it closely. 'Then there's the problem of getting back . . . these bracelets seem to be part of the system. They're obviously designed to fit on the wrist.' He slipped it on and experimentally ran his fingers over a row of studs. 'Part of it looks like it might be a communicator. There's a button here . . . *I don't know what it's for –*'

They both reacted with surprise as Blake's final words echoed loudly round the chamber, issuing from hidden speakers.

'Well, that's it,' Avon affirmed. 'It's tuned to transmit directly to the ship. Probably receives too.'

'Blake!' It was Jenna, who had appeared in the doorway. 'You'd better get up here right away.'

'What is it?'

She looked at him, wide-eyed. 'We've stopped.'

Blake and Avon departed the teleport chamber at the run, following Jenna up to the Flight Deck.

'Did you touch any of the controls?' Blake asked her as they clustered round the flight control position.

Jenna shook her head firmly. 'All of a sudden the indicator

lights started to go out. The needles went back to zero.' She swept her hand across the blank panel. 'It was just like the ship . . . died. Then we stopped,' she finished simply.

'Try the control we used before,' Blake instructed.

Jenna did so and they all turned to the oval grille above which the lights began to flicker in rapid sequence. Then they registered a new pattern and the relays ceased their subdued clicking.

'*State speed and course.*'

'I gave you that,' Blake informed the computer. 'We're supposed to be going to Cygnus Alpha.'

'*That operation has been completed,*' said the soft emotionless voice. '*We are in fixed orbit one thousand spacials above the planet's surface.*'

Blake coughed, slightly disconcerted. 'Oh, all right . . . er, hold that position. Another thing – can we get a look at the planet?'

'*You require the visual receptor circuit?*' Zen enquired tonelessly.

'Yes.' Blake shrugged at the other two. 'At least I think so.'

Behind them, on what they had assumed to be a large featureless expanse of bulkhead, the image of a planet appeared. They turned to look at it, the ominous brooding presence of Cygnus Alpha swathed in drifting layers of mist.

Jenna shivered. 'So that's it. We would have spent the rest of our lives there.'

'The other prisoners will,' Blake told her stonily. 'Unless we do something to help.'

Avon wasn't convinced. 'We don't owe them a thing,' he said indifferently. 'I think we're taking a totally unnecessary risk by coming here. Just because we were all on the same prison ship doesn't obligate us to help them.'

'We couldn't have started the mutiny without them,' Blake pointed out reasonably.

'They knew the chances they were taking. It just happened that we got away and they didn't. If things had been reversed do you think any of them would have come to help us?' Avon's face was a hard unsympathetic mask.

'I don't know,' Blake confessed frankly. 'But my motives aren't entirely unselfish. If we're going to run this ship properly we'll need a crew.' He allowed the silence to linger for a moment. 'And where else are we going to get one?'

'It's a big ship,' Jenna agreed, siding with Blake. 'We'll need all the help we can get.'

'All right then,' Avon said abruptly, though he still didn't sound entirely convinced. 'But just how do you plan to free them?'

Blake turned to stare at the large screen filled with the malevolent image of the misty planet. As if stating an obvious fact, he said mildly, 'One of us has to go down there.'

The prisoners filed down the stone staircase into what Vila could only liken to a pit. It was almost pitch-black, and evil-smelling, and he wondered for a minute if this was to be their final resting-place – until he noticed the heavy iron door at the far end of the gloomy chamber. Behind him, the rest of the prisoners jostled together in the darkness, muttering curses as they stumbled over one another's feet.

Artix stood at the top of the steps, holding a weapon in the crook of his arm, waiting until they were all inside; then without a backward glance he turned and went out, slamming and bolting the transit door, locking them in this dank hole which reeked of sweat, urine and the collective bodily odours of all those other wretches who had passed this way before them.

Vila and Gan wandered forlornly to the iron door, but, as they half expected, it was locked. Vila shrugged his narrow shoulders and twirled round, smiling bleakly.

'Welcome to Cygnus Alpha,' he said in a parody of a toadying lackey. 'And the sumptuous lobby of the famed Starways Hotel. In a moment you will be assigned your luxury suites. Room service is available night and day and our staff will be pleased to provide whatever you require for your pleasure . . . '

'Knock it off, will you!' This from a morose individual, Arco, who fancied himself as a leader of men. Once or twice now he had tried to exert his authority, though no one had paid much attention. He looked round the chamber, his eyes narrowed and rather fearful. 'Why do you suppose they've put us down here?'

'A sort of holding area,' Vila hazarded. 'They'll probably release us by remote-control once the ship is ready for lift-off. But it isn't this place that bothers me – ' he jerked his head to indicate the heavy iron door ' – it's what is on the other side of *that.*'

One of the prisoners, Klein, shuffled his feet restlessly and asked in a quiet voice, 'What do you think it will be like?'

'Not good,' Arco replied, grimacing. 'They don't choose easy living planets to set up prison colonies.'

'Will there be guards?' asked Selman, a short thick-set fellow with a hanging paunch. 'Any kind of authority?'

'They don't need them,' Vila answered. 'A thousand million miles of space makes a pretty good prison wall.'

There was a long uneasy silence while they waited for something to happen. It was the not knowing that scraped at their nerves, made them jumpy and tense.

Selman broke the silence, panting a little with fear. 'Why are they keeping us here?' he demanded anxiously, looking round in the gloom.

'What's your hurry?' Vila squinted at him, his expression comical. 'We're probably in the nicest place on the planet.'

He held up his finger and everyone went very still, as faintly, in the distance, they heard the slow mounting whine of a rocket engine.

'They're getting ready for lift-off,' said Arco in a hushed voice.

They waited tensely, listening as the sound intensified, and then from the iron door there came a distinctive *clunk* which riveted everyone's attention. All eyes were fixed unblinkingly on the door as it slowly creaked open and outside they could see nothing but a dense grey blankness, wisps of chill mist floating like phantoms in the chamber.

Clustering at the entrance, the prisoners stared out into a nightmarish landscape that was all the more terrible for being shrouded in vague drifting banks of fog.

'Cold,' Vila grunted. 'Very cold . . .'

'Can't see much,' Gan ventured, peering into the greyness.

'What is it?' Selman asked, wrinkling his nose as he sniffed the dank air, its touch like a clammy hand on his brow. 'Like something rotting . . .'

'It's death, my friends,' Vila informed them drably. 'The sweet smell of death.'

The whine of the rocket rose suddenly to a shrill piercing crescendo that forced them to cover their ears. The vivid glare as the spacecraft ascended lit the area with a ghostly luminescence that seemed to dance and shimmer on the rolling banks of fog, and as the light and the sound slowly faded Vila clutched at Gan's arm.

'There's someone there . . . look!'

It might have been a trick of the light – yet for the briefest moment it seemed as though a dark hooded figure had been glimpsed through the swirling mist, one arm raised in a beckoning gesture that reminded Vila of the grim reaper enticing them to their doom. But then it was gone, swallowed up, nothing there except shifting greyness.

'Did you see it? Did you?' Vila asked urgently.

'I saw something,' Klein said uncertainly.

The prisoners stared out, none of them eager to make the first move, and it was left to Olag Gan to shoulder his way through. With a terse, 'I'll look,' he marched boldly forward, his tall powerful frame soon lost in the mist and darkness.

The silence pressed heavily, like a tangible if unseen presence.

'Gan ... are you all right?' Arco called softly.

Mist and silence.

'Gan?' Arco's voice heightened with the strain of waiting. He turned to the others. 'He might be in trouble. Come on.'

Vila grabbed him roughly by the arm. 'Wait! Wouldn't it be better if we stayed here? Wait till it gets light?' His gargoyle's face peered up hopefully.

Arco shook him off scornfully and stepped through the doorway, the other prisoners edging after him as if any action was preferable to the waiting, the grey mist, the empty silence.

Vila threw up his hands helplessly and trailed after them. 'I'm not staying here on my own,' he muttered to himself, skipping to catch up.

The group moved forward, clustered tightly together, Arco at its head, and almost immediately was lost in a featureless world without scale or dimensions. It was like being surrounded by an impenetrable grey wall.

Arco moved blindly on and then stiffened as he perceived what he thought was a giant. It was a hooded figure, immensely tall, and it was only when he had ventured a few paces forward that he made it out to be a shrouded body lashed to an arrangement of poles in the shape of a large X – the hands and feet spreadeagled and bound at the wrists and ankles.

Kneeling before this grotesque crucifixion, as if in worship, was Gan, and as they neared him he rose up quickly and turned, holding something.

'What is it?' Arco whispered, straining to see.

Gan held out a piece of rough board. Burned into it was a crude legend which read *So Perish Unbelievers*.

Taking the board, Arco stood looking up at the splayed figure whose face was hidden in the folds of a cowl. Standing

119

on tip-toe, he reached up and used the board to push aside the cowl, revealing what was concealed there . . .

The mummified face of a man, empty sockets staring sightlessly into the mist, teeth locked in a terrible grimace of death.

8

Blake snapped on the metal bracelet and looked across to where Jenna and Avon were leaning over the teleport control panel, their heads close together in rapt concentration. They had hardly moved in the last ten minutes.

'Have you worked it out yet?'

Avon straightened up, frowning slightly. 'I can make some reasonable guesses but I can't be certain,' he said doubtfully.

'Well, the only way we'll find out is by trying,' Blake shrugged.

'I still think it's stupid and dangerous to take the chance,' Avon objected. He shook his head and glanced at Jenna. 'There's nothing that would make me risk it.'

Blake remained indefatigably cheerful. 'Don't worry. If something goes wrong I won't be around to blame you.' He gestured towards the large clockface marked off in coloured segments. 'Time me on that. Give me a count of four minutes. After that, start figuring out how to get me back aboard.'

'Stupid,' Avon mumbled, turning back to the control panel. 'Just stupid.'

Blake winked at Jenna and went across to the row of open-sided cubicles, grouped in a semi-circle.

'Good luck,' she called to him.

'Thanks. Let's try it now.'

Avon's hand hovered tentatively over the controls. After

a momentary hesitation he pressed a button, peering reluctantly over his shoulder as if afraid he might witness some dreadful calamity.

Nothing happened.

'Try again,' Blake said, undaunted.

Avon selected another control, this time with more confidence, and even before he had time to observe what was happening there was an audible gasp from Jenna. Blake was enveloped in a cocoon of shimmering light which grew in intensity until it obliterated him, his body seeming to fragment and dissolve into nothingness. When the glow faded he was gone.

Jenna and Avon exchanged a nervous glance, then she reached out and activated the timing device. 'Starting the count,' she advised Avon, and together they watched as the hand began to sweep round the dial.

For Blake, the experience was less traumatic, even something of an anti-climax. One second he was in the *Liberator*'s teleport area, the next in a dim ethereal landscape, surrounded by the looming shapes of rocks and sparse scrub.

His first thought was one of relief – that he had been teleported intact down to the surface of Cygnus Alpha. Every molecule was still in place, fulfilling its appointed function. He breathed a shallow sigh and looked carefully around, becoming suddenly aware of how cold it was . . . to have spent the rest of his life on this dark, dank, forbidding world! No wonder some dissidents preferred death to deportation.

A sound alerted him and he held his breath, straining to hear. Footsteps approaching from – which direction? He couldn't be sure. The surrounding mist muffled and distorted the crunch of gravel so that it was in front and behind and all around at the same time.

He crept into the shelter of a large rock, recoiling from its chill, slimy feel. The footsteps had stopped. There was someone nearby, very close perhaps, he felt it in his bones, and the instinct made him spin round to see a pair of clawlike hands reaching for his throat. Cowering against the rock, he made out the silhouette of a hooded figure bending towards him, scrawny arms outstretched in a deathly embrace. The hands came nearer, nails like talons, and as they were about to grip him he held up his arm defensively and through the crook of his elbow saw Jenna's relieved and delighted face.

'We got you back!' she exclaimed, rushing forward to embrace him.

'It worked!' Avon said, sounding more surprised than anything else.

Blake moved away from the transmission area, his knees decidedly weak.

'I was frightened out of my mind,' Jenna chattered, hugging his arm.

'It's all right,' Blake assured them, realising that it was. 'I'm fine.'

'What was it like?' Jenna asked excitedly.

'I'm not exactly sure.' He frowned as he tried to recall. 'There's no particular sensation. You're just suddenly in another place . . .'

Avon scratched his chin, lost in admiration for the superlative technology that lay all around them like the contents of an Aladdin's Cave. 'It's an astonishing piece of equipment,' he said reverently. 'There's nothing in the known worlds that can actually teleport living matter.'

'It really took you down there!' Jenna squealed, a child thrilled with a new toy. 'On to the surface of Cygnus.'

'Did you see anything?' Avon asked.

Blake didn't answer right away, going to the rack where the bracelets were displayed. 'Not too much,' he said evasively. 'But now we know how the system operates I'll go back down and find our people and bring back anybody who wants to come.' He had taken down ten bracelets and slipped them into his pocket. Glancing meaningfully at Jenna and Avon, he added, 'From the little I saw they'll be glad to get away.'

The spire rose out of the murk like the prow of a sailing ship seen dimly through Arctic mists. It was a monumental edifice that instantly reminded Vila of a place of pagan worship – huge and yet crudely constructed in the manner of a primitive people.

The group had halted at the sight of this strange pointed structure, staying close together in a tight defensive knot.

'What do you think it is?' Klein asked apprehensively.

'I wonder who built it?' Vila mused aloud, which concerned him more than its purpose. Buildings meant people.

'That's not important,' Arco rapped, still trying to prove that he possessed the decisive qualities of leadership. 'We may find food and shelter there.'

He was about to carry on when a movement caught his eye and he touched Gan's arm, pointing a little way ahead. 'I could have sworn . . .'

And then there was no mistake as first one hooded figure glided silently from out of the darkness to stand in front of them, to be joined by another, and another, and yet another, until finally thirty or so had formed an arc, each one garbed in the same anonymous habit, their faces hidden by the deep cowls.

They remained thus, motionless, confronting the prisoners, and there was something menacing about them even though they displayed no overt aggression.

The central figure stepped forward and came – purposely it seemed – to stand directly in front of Gan. The broad-shouldered young man looked down on the figure, unafraid, and when he spoke his voice was firm, almost defiant.

'Who are you?' he demanded.

'I am the servant of your God,' came the soft insidious reply.

Hands reached up and pushed back the cowl to reveal Kara's evil, haunting beauty – a face that was disfigured by a kind of lustful greed. Thrusting her arms towards him, palms splayed open, she took Gan's face gently between her hands and with a swift savage movement pulled his head forward and kissed him full on the mouth.

With a smile that was rapturous and yet somehow obscene, she greeted them joyfully. 'Welcome, brothers! Come, follow us . . . God has prepared a place for you.'

Leading the way, Kara beckoned them to follow, and the prisoners shuffled after her, Vila noting with some small disquiet that during this the hooded figures had closed ranks and were now in front, on both sides, and also behind them.

'I think we've got some of this figured out,' Avon told Blake as they stood at the teleport control panel. 'Transmit and receive are fairly straightforward. I think the rest of the controls are directional. Once we've got it right I'd say we could teleport you to a precise geographical point.'

'When we have some time we'll run some experiments.' Blake made one final check on his equipment and moved across to the transmission area. 'I'm all set.'

'How long do you want this time?'

'Give me four Earth hours. That should be enough.' He tapped the bracelet on his wrist. 'If there's any change I'll contact you on this.'

Avon looked up from the control panel. 'What if something happens?' he asked worriedly. 'Supposing we don't hear from you or we can't get you back aboard?'

Blake regarded him soberly. 'Use your own judgement. But I wouldn't want you to move off too soon . . . ' he said gently, leaving the inference hanging in the air.

'What do you think we are?' Avon protested. 'We wouldn't leave you stuck down there!' He was scandalised by the very idea.

'That's nice to know.' Blake squared his shoulders and nodded sharply. 'All right. Let's get on with it.'

He saw Avon reach out to the control panel and a moment later the scene underwent a rapid transformation: the brightly-lit teleport area faded from view to be replaced by a rough stone wall marked with ancient carvings. In the pale light of dawn he could make out the dark bulk of a building rising above him, a temple of some kind judging by the style of architecture.

Moving cautiously along and keeping close to the wall, he came eventually to a large wooden door set deeply into the stonework, a heavy iron ring serving as a handle. Blake listened intently, and after satisfying himself that all was quiet, eased the door open and slipped inside.

His first impression had been right. The interior comprised a high vaulted chamber supported by crude stone columns, the whole of this dimly illuminated by flickering torches and bowls of burning oil. Tapestries woven with strange symbols covered the rough stone walls, and at the head of the chamber an altar had been constructed out of huge stone slabs above which an ornamental throne, carved with the same mysterious symbols, surveyed the silent, heavily-shadowed chamber.

Blake advanced slowly towards the altar, nagged by vague puzzling doubts. Without any question this was a place of worship, yet he couldn't remember ever having heard of a native population on Cygnus Alpha. Then who had been responsible for the construction of the temple? And what kind of religion did they practise in this forgotten corner of the outer systems?

He was about to examine some of the objects which lay on the altar – stone artefacts, a beaten copper chalice, an earthenware bowl inlaid with semi-precious stones – when the sound of shuffling footsteps alerted him. Moving into the shadow of one of the columns, he watched intrigued as a woman entered from a side door and knelt before the throne. The hood of her robe was thrown back and in the shifting light he saw a face that was suffused with a kind of sly malevolence, beautiful and yet chilling in its evil intent.

Her pale hands moved gracefully in a series of symbolic

gestures and when this small ceremony was over she bowed low, her forehead almost touching the flagged floor, and from behind a tapestry to one side of the throne a man appeared – tall and solidly-built with fair curly hair that surrounded his head like a halo. Although extremely handsome, his face had an arrogant leer, superior and disdainful. His robe was similar to that of the woman's, though of a finer weave, and in his belt a broad-bladed knife caught and reflected the torchlight.

Raising his arms high, the man intoned solemnly, 'His blessings are upon you. Speak and He will hear you.'

'I am His true servant,' the woman answered reverently, lifting her head to gaze upon him, her eyes like lustrous black pools.

'The souls from the outer darkness are among us?'

'They are in the place of novices.'

'How do they number?'

'They are thirty.'

The fair-haired man permitted himself a cold, humourless smile. 'A true bounty. Have they been touched by the Death?'

'The Curse of Cygnus is upon them all.'

'Then let them know His mercy. Teach them the first law.'

The woman's face was devoid of all expression as she repeated tonelessly, ' "Only from His hand comes life. Only from His wrath comes death. We obey Him and give thanks for His mercy." '

Moving with slow, dignified steps, as if part of some elaborate ritual, the man went to a small cupboard with carved doors set in the rear wall and with a large key hung around his neck removed a small ornate casket which he brought forward. The woman had risen and taken a silver salver from the altar; she held it up to him with outstretched arms. With due ceremony the man lifted the lid of the casket, took a handful of small white tablets, and sprinkled them into the salver. Setting the casket down, his hands moved in

127

mystical gestures over the salver, his head thrown back while he pronounced the blessing.

'He is the giver of salvation. His power drives away the wild beast that is death. It is He who must be obeyed.'

'We thank Him,' the woman responded, bowing and retreating a few paces. Holding the salver before her, she turned and left the chamber by the same door she had entered, whereupon the man returned the casket to the cupboard and disappeared behind the tapestry.

The chamber was silent and deserted once more.

Blake stepped out from the shadow of the stone pillar. The prisoners were here, that much was evident, but where exactly? Treading carefully, he crossed the vaulted chamber to the side door through which the woman had just departed. There was a grille. He peered through.

Avon was explaining to Jenna how the teleport transmission system worked. He was reasonably confident that he had figured it out. 'As far as I can see, it has a maximum range of about fifteen hundred spacials.'

'What would happen if you transmitted someone when you were outside that distance from a planet?' Jenna wanted to know.

'I imagine they would break down into molecules in the same way but never reassemble. They'd become millions of sub-atoms and be scattered all over the Universe.'

'Dust to dust . . . ' Jenna murmured. She smiled brightly and set off for the door. 'I think I'll do a little exploring. It doesn't need two of us here.'

Avon nodded. 'Fine with me.'

'Give me a call if you hear anything from Blake.'

'I don't expect anything for a while,' Avon replied, glancing up at the sweeping hand on the large timing device. 'Unless there's an emergency.'

The light from a single torch was barely enough to illuminate the shallow flight of stone steps leading down to a narrow passageway. Peering through the grille, Blake could just make out a table and chair in the flickering gloom, but nothing beyond.

He thought, *In for a penny* . . . and was about to try his luck when the woman came into view, accompanied by another robed figure. She carried the silver salver, which was now empty. They paused by the table, the man reaching out to hang a heavy bunch of keys on a wooden peg.

Blake strained to hear.

' . . . the sickness will end soon,' the woman was saying. 'When it does, He will come to them.'

The man nodded, his face haggard and wild, his hair a shaggy mane. 'With new souls to do His work there will be chances for us . . . for the faithful to rise to priesthood.'

'He will not fail us,' the woman assured him in a vehement whisper. 'We will be rewarded.'

She turned and came swiftly up the steps, and Blake, caught unawares, looked round in sudden panic for a place of concealment. There was none. Pressing himself flat against the stonework, he saw the door swing open towards him, and then she had passed through without a sideways glance and in a moment had disappeared into the shadowed depths of the chamber.

Blake breathed a silent prayer. Waiting until his heart had steadied, he risked a look through the grille and saw that the man had seated himself at the table, his back to the door. Easing the door open, Blake slipped inside and flattened himself against the wall; holding his breath, he edged slowly down the steps.

The man appeared to be dozing. Could he risk getting past him without being seen? Blake wondered, and decided he couldn't. There was a way – perhaps the only way – and Blake knew he had to take the chance. Covering his hand with his sleeve, he reached up and snuffed out the flame that

9   129

burned in the single torch clamped to the wall. The passageway was plunged into darkness.

There was a wearisome grunt, the scrape of a chair, and feet shuffled on the flagged floor. A moment later, the sound of a flint being struck on metal . . . and as the torch was ignited Blake vanished beyond into the enveloping gloom.

Walking on tiptoe, all his senses alert, he came eventually to a heavy wooden door bound with iron strips, the first of several such doors in the wall of the passageway. Muffled sounds of coughing came from inside, and fainter still, the low moaning of men in pain.

Blake opened the small hinged panel and stared in through the barred opening. The cell contained about ten prisoners, all of them in the indolent attitude of the sick, lying on the floor or propped against the walls, their faces running with sweat, their breathing hoarse and rapid. One or two seemed to be in the grip of coma, staring sightlessly into space.

Near the door, on a low trestle-bed, Blake saw the unmistakable figure of Olag Gan, his head buried in his hands. Lifting his mouth to the bars, Blake called to him in a low, urgent voice.

It took some time for the big man to respond. He looked up blearily and a slow shock of recognition passed across his face. He climbed unsteadily to his feet and lurched towards the door. 'Blake . . . ?'

'What is it?' Blake hissed. 'What's the matter with everybody?'

Only now had Gan come back to himself. 'How did you get here?'

Blake shook his head impatiently. 'Never mind that now. *What's wrong?*'

'A disease . . . ' Gan moistened his parched lips. 'Something in the atmosphere of this planet. All new arrivals here suffer it.'

'Can it be treated?'

'They've given us a drug,' Gan nodded. 'The priests say we will recover quickly.'

'Why are they keeping you prisoners?'

'We're not prisoners. They're just keeping us confined until we get well. They've been good to us. We've had food and drink and been well looked after.'

'All right.' Blake's tone changed, became brisk. 'Now listen to me. We've got a spacecraft. Jenna and Avon are waiting on board. There's a chance that I can get those who want to come up to her. After that we can go anywhere –'

'But we can't leave!'

Gan's stricken face was framed in the small opening, sweat gleaming on his neck.

'What are you talking about?' Blake asked, frowning.

'I told you – the sickness. We are all infected with the sickness.'

Blake didn't understand. 'But you've been given the drug . . .'

'Don't you see?' Gan said hoarsely. He stared through the bars and mouthed slowly. 'It can't be cured.' He shook his head, his eyes filled with pain. 'We're infected now. To stay alive we have to be treated with the drug every day for the rest of our lives. If we leave here we will die.'

The meaning of what he was saying slowly filtered through. Blake said in a half-whisper, 'And everybody has contracted the disease?'

'Everybody,' Gan affirmed. 'The priests told us that every human to come here is victim to the sickness. They call it the Curse of Cygnus. No one is immune.'

'Then why hasn't it affected me?' Blake asked curiously.

'It will. It comes with great speed. We were all struck down with it less than two hours after we set foot here.'

'I've been here almost that long myself,' Blake said thoughtfully.

'Then it's already in your system. The symptoms will show soon. If you go back to your ship you will take the sickness with you . . . contaminate Avon and Jenna.'

Blake's mind raced as he sought to find a way out of the dilemma. Was it really true that he had been infected with some dread disease and was forced to remain on this hell-hole of a planet for the rest of his life? What superb irony if he had escaped the prison ship only to have walked voluntarily into another, much more deadly trap. Was he even yet a prisoner as they were?

'Listen, I'll talk with the leaders,' he told Gan, sounding more cheerful than he felt. 'They can give us a supply of the drug or tell us how it's made. In return I can offer some of them a chance to get away from here.'

Gan brightened a little at the prospect. Perhaps there was still a chance after all. 'It's possible,' he agreed hopefully. 'They might agree.'

'I'll see what can be done,' Blake promised. 'You rest now. I'll see you later.' He smiled reassuringly and closed the hinged panel.

His mind still in a turmoil of seeking a solution to the problem, Blake turned away from the door, and was allowed the tiniest fraction of a second to register the two hooded figures standing directly behind him before a great weight seemed to descend from the sky, crushing his skull flat, and the inside of his brain exploded. He had lapsed into merciful unconsciousness before the pain had time to hit him.

Avon yawned and rubbed his eyes with his knuckles, bored with the inactivity and the waiting. Sitting back with his feet propped up on the teleport control panel, he roused enough energy to glance at the timing device, then once again lapsed into dozing reverie. He had just figured out the perfect fool-proof method of embezzling five million credits from the Federation banking system when Jenna appeared in the doorway and softly called his name.

Avon casually looked round and then sat up straight, his

eyes popping out of his head. His first thought was to wonder how a beautiful and sexy star maiden had managed to get aboard the *Liberator* and it took all of ten seconds for him to realise that it was Jenna, attired in the most magnificent – and rather revealing – space-age costume.

She stood in the doorway, well aware of the stunning effect and revelling in Avon's goggling admiration, her expression one of impish seductiveness.

'That looks – ' Avon swallowed ' – incredible.' He got slowly to his feet and gazed at her with real appreciation.

'You think it does something for me?' Jenna enquired coyly, posing for him.

Avon nodded dumbly. 'It does something for me too,' he confessed.

'It's been a long time since I wore clothes like this. It makes me feel like a woman again.'

'It doesn't leave too much doubt about that,' Avon told her truthfully. 'Where did you get it?'

She gestured vaguely. 'I found a whole room down there . . . just filled with clothes. Hundreds of things,' she added, twirling round delightedly.

'Men's things too?'

'Yes,' Jenna smiled brightly.

'I could stand a change from this,' Avon grimaced, looking down at his drab prison coverall.

'Go down – I'll take over here for a while.'

'Thanks.' He started for the door.

'Avon.'

He paused by the door. 'Yes?'

She let a moment elapse and then said in a rather distant tone of voice. 'There's another room you should see while you're down there. The door at the furthest end of the passage.' She looked at him with a curious expression. 'You might find it interesting . . . '

'What's in it?' Avon said, intrigued.

'Rare stones,' Jenna said quietly. 'Precious metals. Currency from various planets. A fortune . . . a great, great fortune.'

Avon pursed his lips, his eyes locked on hers. Then abruptly he left the room and Jenna stared after him, her expression thoughtful and serious.

Vargas stood before the altar, his cruel, arrogant face framed by curled golden locks upturned as if in silent homage to a mysterious deity. He was thinking slyly that this was the greatest opportunity of all; he had known that one day it would come, and here it was at last. The new star in the heavens promised the fulfilment of all his dreams.

The man lying at his feet stirred and sat up, rubbing his head. Vargas turned and looked down on him, his lips curving in a mocking smile.

'You are recovered?'

'Just about.' Blake opened his eyes painfully and tentatively touched his scalp, feeling for the lump that was throbbing with a dull sickly ache.

Vargas gestured brusquely to the two hooded figures standing nearby. 'Leave us.' They bowed and shuffled off into the darkness of the chamber.

Blake climbed to his feet, and as he straightened up his hand went instinctively to his waist.

'You were looking for this?' Vargas held up the belt with its holstered handgun. 'An interesting design,' he mused. 'A weapon of some kind. You will instruct me in its use.'

'I'm not too certain about it myself,' Blake told him truthfully. Something else occurred to him and he was about to check the contents of his pockets when, with a sweeping motion, Vargas threw back a cloth on the altar to reveal a pile of bracelets.

'We also relieved you of your other possessions,' Vargas informed him silkily.

134

Blake grasped at his wrist and his heart sank. That bracelet too was missing.

'I found these fascinating,' Vargas continued smoothly. 'Some sort of body adornment I thought at first.' He selected one from the pile and held it delicately between his fingertips. 'Then I wondered why a man would carry so many of them in his pocket. Perhaps for trade? Or to use in barter? But then I thought again and that didn't seem to be the answer.'

His tone was light, unhurried, speculative, but his eyes were shrewd and watchful.

Blake shrugged dismissively and strove to keep his voice unconcerned. 'They have no value in themselves.'

Vargas smiled and nodded, quite prepared, it seemed, to accept this. Watching Blake's face, he took the bracelet in both hands and with cold deliberation twisted and bent the metal until it snapped in two. He tossed the pieces aside and picked up another bracelet.

'How did you come here?' he asked casually, toying with the bracelet.

'I was a prisoner on the Federation ship.'

Vargas smiled again, almost apologetically, and as if it were of no consequence twisted and snapped the bracelet. 'That is untrue,' he said reproachfully, throwing the pieces aside. 'The prisoners were observed from the moment they landed. All are accounted for.'

He picked up another bracelet. Blake took a deep calming breath.

'So when an extra soul was discovered, I became puzzled,' Vargas went on, gripping the bracelet. 'Then I saw the new star in our firmament. It was then that things began to become clear to me.' His hands tightened and began to twist the metal. 'It is a spacecraft, isn't it?' he said, his voice gaining a strident note.

'Don't destroy any more of those,' Blake implored him, making as if to step forward.

'Then answer.' Vargas' eyes had narrowed. He waited.

'Yes,' Blake admitted reluctantly. 'It is a spacecraft. But what I said is true – I was a Federation prisoner. With two others I escaped. We took control of a ship and came here to take off any of the prisoners who wanted to come.'

Vargas regarded him suspiciously, but there must have been something in Blake's manner that apparently satisfied him. 'It seems unlikely but it has the ring of truth,' he said finally.

Blake watched the tall, golden-haired man and was relieved to see him slacken his grip. He twirled the bracelet in his fingers, studying it, and then on a whim slipped it on to his wrist. Taking the handgun from its holster, the coiled cable attached to the power unit in the belt, he examined the weapon closely, seemingly fascinated by such advanced technology, and after a moment pointed it carelessly in Blake's direction. Speaking in an easy, conversational tone, he began to recite what sounded like an oft-repeated liturgy:

'I am the supreme power here. My word is the law. My followers obey without question. They worship me because I am life and I am death.'

'Do they really worship you?' Blake asked with veiled scepticism. 'Or is it just fear?'

'The motive is not important,' Vargas said indifferently.

'Why you?'

'Because I am directly descended in the true and chosen line. Mine is the power by right.'

Again it was said with such bland familiarity that it might have been spoken by rote.

'What right?' Blake demanded. 'Listen, two hundred years ago this planet was uninhabited. Then the Federation decided to use it as a Penal Colony and transported the first batch of fifty criminals.' He raised one eyebrow in sardonic disbelief. 'Is that the noble line you stem from?'

'My great-great-grandfather came here in that first shipment,' Vargas said in a low, intense voice. 'They had nothing.

136

The Federation gave them no supplies, no tools, so they worked together, worked hard, made a community. There were children born here. They were the first real settlers trying to build a life for themselves on a new planet. Later, more Federation prisoners came. There were disagreements. The community began to break into small groups. They fought . . . they killed . . . and all they had achieved was being destroyed.' His voice took on a new note, became imbued with mystical fervour. 'It was my great-grandfather who found the way to unite them. He taught them a religion. Brought them together in the love and fear of one Almighty God. *That* is the line I stem from! *That* is what gives me the right to rule!'

He had worked himself up to fever-pitch, his nostrils flaring with the fierce emotion of his avowed belief that he ruled by divine right. It was clear that Vargas regarded every word as the gospel truth.

Blake was uncomfortably aware that the handgun was still loosely aimed in his direction. With commendable regard for his own self-preservation, he adopted a pacifying line.

'Look, I'm sorry . . , I had no knowledge of the history of Cygnus. I had no right to question your authority. I apologise.'

Vargas had become calmer now, his face more composed. 'You are wise. Unbelievers perish in his wrath,' he pronounced.

Blake decided that this approach was the wisest under the circumstances. 'When I came here I had no intention of disrupting or interfering with your way of life. I wanted only to offer the chance of freedom to some of the new prisoners. Now they are victims of a disease. I understand you have a drug that will combat it.'

Vargas nodded slowly, his eyes fixed on Blake. 'They will require it each day for the rest of their lives.'

'Then I ask that you allow the men to decide which of them want to come with me.' Blake's voice was quiet, reasonable in tone, one intelligent man asking a favour of another. 'Give me a supply of the drug, or the formula –'

'No.'

'I need those men,' Blake insisted firmly. 'I must have a crew.'

'No!' Vargas jerked his head savagely. 'This society needs people. New blood. Muscle and sinew to work the land. Human souls are the only currency, the only capital on this planet. Our God is bankrupt without them.'

'All right.' Blake tried another tack. 'Will you trade them? There must be something on my ship that you could use –'

Vargas picked up a bracelet and threw it down in disgust, as if it were a cheap trinket. 'Toys like these . . . ' he said scornfully, and held up the handgun ' . . . or this? Are these what you are offering me?'

'Tell me what you want.'

'The only wealth I know is power.'

'And that you already have.'

'Here, yes,' Vargas agreed craftily. He stared into the darkness of the chamber, his eyes gleaming with the magnitude of his aspirations. 'But to take the Word beyond . . . to gather followers in new worlds. New disciples bound together and obeying the one true God . . . '

He raised his curled hand, as if reaching for the stars, and then turned on Blake with the full fervour of religious fanaticism. 'That is what I want!' he blazed. 'That is what you will give me!!'

'How?' Blake was plainly bewildered.

'Your ship!' Vargas spat at him. 'You will give me your ship!'

'No –'

'It is my command,' Vargas said imperiously. 'You will contact your ship and order it to land.'

Blake shook his head defiantly. 'I can't do that. I won't.'

'Oh no,' said Vargas with menacing softness. 'You are mistaken.'

He snapped his fingers and from the surrounding darkness emerged three hooded figures. With brute force two of them grabbed Blake's arms while the third locked a forearm across his throat, holding him fast and helpless.

'He has defied the Word,' Vargas said tonelessly, his voice drab, empty. 'Teach him the meaning of obedience.'

Blake released a strangled gasp of pain as he was dragged backwards into the shadows.

For a little while longer Vargas stood by the altar, toying with the bracelets, watching how the torchlight glinted on the smooth burnished metal. He paused to listen to the unidentifiable sounds which reached him from the darkness, rather pleased when they increased in pitch and intensity and echoed round the gloomy chamber, smiling to himself with quiet satisfaction.

Eventually, having heard enough, he tossed the bracelet on to the pile and moved towards the large entrance door, the dull blows and muffled groans diminishing and gradually fading away as he stepped outside to join Kara, her head thrown back, gazing raptly into the night sky. He too looked upwards, seeing the new star which outshone all the rest, gleaming like a fixed brilliant beacon in the heavens.

Kara's voice was hushed with the awesome splendour of it. 'Is it a sign?' she asked tremulously.

'Yes,' Vargas answered dreamily. 'It tells us the time has come to take our truth out into the Universe. Time to show new worlds the power of the true Word.'

They gazed at it in reverent silence.

Vargas said, 'The unbeliever will not submit easily. He will not learn obedience quickly. We must use other . . . persuasions.'

And as he continued to watch the bright new star an idea formed in his mind. Leaning towards Kara, he spoke softly in her ear. 'Go to the place of novices,' he instructed. 'Speak to those who have newly come to us. Tell them . . .'

And she too smiled as his meaning was made clear to her.

139

Nodding her understanding, Kara turned and glided away, silent as a wraith.

Vargas looked once again into the night sky, well pleased with the scheme the new star had inspired in him. It was indeed a sign . . . of the unimaginable power granted Him.

The star. The spacecraft. The *Liberator*.

9

The sun of the Cygnus Alpha system threw a hard glare of light against the hull of the *Liberator* as she hung, seemingly motionless, above the misty planet. The auto-navigational computer had taken every factor into account – gravitational force, spin, orbital drift, angular momentum – and processed these data to provide the ship's electro-gyro facility with precise co-ordinates to maintain her position. Thus she turned with the planet, always at a fixed point in relation to its surface.

In the teleport section, Jenna fretted with impatience as she watched the large hand sweep round the segmented face of the timing device. She had agreed with Blake that they needed extra people to crew the ship, but was it worth the risk of remaining in such close proximity to the prison planet? She was beginning to have grave doubts.

After twenty minutes or so, Avon returned. He seemed dazed by what he had found, entering the section clutching bundles of banknotes, jewellery and precious stones which he held out to her in mute wonder.

'You know how much is here?' he asked after a moment, his voice strained with incredulity, spreading the money and valuables across the control console.

'Tell me,' Jenna said, trying to resist the temptation of running her fingers over the jewellery. It sparkled and caught her eye in beautiful glittering profusion.

'More than five million credits in Federation currency.' Avon gazed at it as if he couldn't believe his eyes. 'And this is just the beginning. There must be thousands of millions stored down there. And not just Federation currency . . . every sort. There are precious metals, some I've never ever seen before. There's more wealth in that single room than I can begin to comprehend.'

He was completely bowled over by the immensity of this vast treasure.

'You could buy a lot of freedom with that much,' Jenna said abstractedly, her fingers straying towards the jewellery.

'You could buy *anything* with that much,' Avon retorted eagerly. 'Anything we wanted for the rest of our lives. Think of that, Jenna . . . there'd be nothing you couldn't have!'

'Enough for all of us?'

'All?' Avon became very still. He was holding a small, perfectly formed ruby, studying it with intense concentration.

'Blake and whoever he brings back with him.'

Avon didn't answer. His eyes came up to meet hers and she saw instantly, knew without any doubt, what was written there. She was shocked and reacted vehemently.

'Leave him here?' Jenna said, outraged. 'No!'

'Why not?'

'We can't.'

'Listen, Jenna . . . ' His voice softened persuasively. 'We've got a chance here that might never come again. You could go off to a neutral planet somewhere, set yourself up in a beautiful home, have anything you want and never ask the cost. Think of it . . . '

Jenna's fingers touched the jewellery, stroked it. Now that Avon had implanted the idea she was beginning to see its appeal. How easy it would be. All her problems solved by one swift decisive act. And yet . . .

Avon pressed on, knowing she was swayed. 'If we stay with Blake all we have to look forward to is trekking round the Universe while he runs a crusade against the Federation. We'll be on the run all the time. Federation Security ships will come after us and sooner or later they're bound to catch up with us.' His voice hardened, became more insistent. 'We'll get no mercy from them. They'll destroy us – they have to. Is that what you want?'

Avon's large pale eyes watched her unblinkingly and Jenna had to avert her gaze. Her face was troubled, uncertain.

'I just don't like the idea of leaving him down there,' she countered hesitantly.

'We'll never have this chance again,' he persisted.

Jenna bit her lip. She fondled the jewellery, then came quickly to a decision. 'An hour. We'll wait one hour,' she told him firmly. 'If we've heard nothing by then we'll leave.'

'But why?' Avon spread his hands, obviously perplexed, unable to see the logic. 'Why wait?'

'Because that way I can convince myself we gave him a fair chance.' Jenna looked directly at him, spots of colour burning in her cheeks. 'But if he's not back by then, we leave.'

They looked up to the large hand as it swept inexorably round the clockface.

Blake swam back to consciousness through a sea of pain. The followers of the cult had received expert instruction in the manner and means of instilling obedience into believers. Yet Blake felt far from obedient. Until now he had been prepared to make his demands in a reasonable fashion, but it seemed that the time of reason was passed. Vargas understood nothing except power; it was a philosophy whose real meaning would have to be brought home to him.

Struggling to sit up, Blake reached out for support to the other prisoners who stood in a sullen group on the far side of the cell. Strangely, it seemed that none of them wished to come near him. Blinking in the dim light, Blake called out to the man nearest him:

'Arco, give me a hand, will you?'

Arco made no move. He glowered at Blake as if he were an outcast.

'What is it?' Blake asked, getting painfully to his feet. He looked from Arco to the others, all silent, unmoving. 'What's the matter with you? Gan? Vila?'

'You have to give them what they want, Blake.' Arco spoke harshly, a command rather than a plea.

'What are you talking about?' Blake said incredulously. He shook his fists at them. 'That madman wants the ship! Do you understand? Give him that and we're finished!'

'We're finished anyway,' Arco snapped.

'They refuse to give us the drug unless you do as they order,' Vila explained grimly. 'Without it we will die.'

'Go on,' Arco prompted him, his face a stolid mask. 'Tell him the rest of it.'

'If you delay, one of us will be chosen for sacrifice.'

Blake looked at them silently, his jaw clenching in anger and frustration. So Vargas had played his trump card – succeeded in casting him in the role of the man who held all their lives in his hands. It was a neat and effective ploy, alienating him from his fellow prisoners, who of course would demand that he relinquish command of the ship at once. They valued their lives more than the *Liberator*, even though it might be the most advanced spacecraft in all the Universe.

Arco stepped forward menacingly. 'We're not going to let that happen, Blake.' He flexed his neck pugnaciously, raising his fists in a threatening manner. 'If they can't convince you, then we will ...'

His shoulders slumping wearily, Blake bowed his head, nodding in submission. He was totally defeated at last. The prisoners relaxed, so it came as a complete surprise when without the slightest hint of warning Blake suddenly uncoiled like a steel spring and drove his fist hard into Arco's stomach, and as the burly man doubled up aimed a blow which connected cleanly with the point of his jaw and sent him reeling back against the cell wall. Almost in the same movement, Blake snatched up a heavy wooden stool and held it high above his head with both hands, defying any of them to come for him.

His face was livid. His eyes burned with contempt.

None of them seemed eager to be the first.

'You don't deserve to get out of here,' he spat at them disdainfully. 'I should leave you to rot and spend the rest of your lives working in the fields like animals – to live in fear that if you make one wrong move Vargas will cut off your supply of drugs or maybe just on a whim choose one of you for sacrifice.' He curled his lip, looking from one to the other. 'You want to live like that, then fine. But not me. I'm getting out of here or I'll die trying. If you don't have the guts or the intelligence to see that that's the only way, then I wouldn't want you with me anyway.'

His fierce passion shamed them into abject silence. Not one of them would meet his eye. They knew he spoke the truth. Then Vila said:

'I'd risk it, Blake – ' he shrugged ' – but even if we do make it up to the ship we won't have the drug – '

Blake cut him short. 'I know where it's kept. I saw him take it from a box.'

'Enough to keep us all alive?' asked Arco sullenly, rubbing his stomach.

'Listen . . . ' Blake tossed the stool into a corner and faced them. 'That ship up there is the most advanced design in the Universe. There'll be medicines on board, a laboratory. We can analyse the drug and find something like it or manufacture it ourselves.'

He regarded them challengingly, forcing them to decide. One or two seemed undecided, wanting to believe him yet still not entirely convinced.

10

'I don't know . . . ' Arco mumbled hesitantly, glancing at the others.

'In a little while they're going to come and take one of you away,' Blake told them forcefully, spelling it out, making it as plain as he could. 'That one, whoever he is, is going to be killed in some crazy sacrificial ceremony. And let me tell you right now: there's nothing you can say to me – nothing you can do – that will make me order that ship to land. The only choice you have is rotting here or taking a chance and fighting your way out.'

He had done all he could. The rest lay in their hands.

Gan shouldered his way forward, his broad muscular frame as strong and steady as a rock.

'I'm with you.'

Selman nodded and he too came forward.

'Right.' Blake's eyes narrowed. 'Who else?'

The belt and handgun gave Vargas a tremendous feeling of power. In a strange way the thrill was akin to that of sexual ecstasy. He swaggered about in front of the altar, the belt slung low on his hips, relishing the solid heavy compactness of the weapon. The bracelet too fascinated him, even though he did not know its purpose. He looked at it admiringly and decided that from now on these artefacts of an alien civilisation would be part of his ceremonial dress, symbols of the new power he was about to attain.

The sound of a gong reverberated through the chamber and Kara appeared from out of the shadows. She placed a large double-edged blade on the altar and bowed before it.

'It is time,' she informed him solemnly.

'Bring the chosen one to the place of sacrifice,' Vargas commanded.

Kara left the chamber, followed by several hooded figures.

Vargas took the weapon from its holster, uncoiling the

cable, and adjusted the calibrated controls in an experimental way. Holding it at arm's length and sighting along the barrel, he tentatively pressed the button trigger, aiming casually at one of the stone pillars, and nearly dropped the handgun in alarm when there was a jagged flash of brilliant blue light and a rippling energy-wave erupted from the muzzle and blew a large section of the pillar into tiny pulverised fragments.

When the smoke and dust had subsided he hurried across to examine the damage in more detail. The stonework was seared and pitted from the blast, as though subjected to an incredibly high temperature, and Vargas gazed at the weapon in his hand with a mixture of amazement and respect. Never before had he come across anything that could annihilate matter with such savage force; with such power nothing could stand in his way.

He held the weapon as if it were the sacred symbol of his inalienable right to immortal rule. As indeed it was.

Vila peered through the barred opening, then skipped back nimbly to join Blake and those few others who had decided to throw in their lot with him. Altogether they numbered five – and no amount of persuasion could entice the rest to join forces with them.

'They're coming!' Vila whispered, sneaking behind Gan's broad back.

Blake looked across to the other prisoners, clustered in the far corner. 'Your last chance,' he offered them tersely. There was no movement.

Shuffling footsteps from the corridor and the sound of a key being fitted into the lock.

Blake glanced swiftly at his own group, their faces tense with the strain.

'Ready?'

The key grated in the lock.

They nodded, crouching in readiness as the door swung open.

Avon paced nervously to and fro, every few seconds looking impatiently at the face of the timing device. Unable to contain himself any longer, he broke off in mid-stride and spun round to confront Jenna.

'Come on, let's go!' he urged her fiercely. 'There's no point in waiting any longer.'

Jenna's face was pale yet calm. 'There's still six minutes.'

'Look, we've made the decision,' Avon ground out, fuming at the delay. 'Let's just get away from here!'

Jenna lifted her head and gazed directly at him. She had made a pledge with herself and it couldn't be broken. 'We'll wait it out,' she said, speaking quietly but firmly.

Olag Gan was the chosen one. He was marched into the chamber and brought before the altar where, flanked by several members of the faith, Vargas waited with folded arms, his head of golden curls uplifted, his eyes cold and utterly ruthless as they passed fleetingly over the first sacrificial victim. The leader of the prisoners, this fellow Blake, would soon see the error of his ways as one by one his comrades fell victim to the ceremonial blade. Vargas was supremely confident that the remaining prisoners would find the means to make him see.

'The novices made an attack upon us,' reported one of the escort. 'We were able to overcome them.'

'They will be punished,' Vargas answered, taking the double-edged blade from the altar and holding it upright before him. Turning to face Gan, his lips mimed the opening words of the brief ceremony which preceded the moment of sacrifice. The time was almost here.

From one of the hooded figures came a single, softly-spoken word.

'Now,' said the voice of Blake.

Starting back in shocked disbelief, Vargas saw the escort throw off their robes to reveal Blake and three of the prisoners, and even before he knew what was happening Gan had leapt forward, wrenched the blade from his hands and sent him sprawling with a blow that nearly dislocated his jaw.

Blake and the others had been just as quick to take action. Using the element of surprise as their greatest ally, they launched an attack and in seconds the chamber was a battle-ground as men grappled beneath the flickering torchlight in fierce hand-to-hand combat.

Gan joined the fray, taking on two at once, and Blake saw his opportunity. Leaping over a prone body, he ran to the altar and scooped up the bracelets, slipped one on to his wrist, and swiftly distributed the rest to his fellow prisoners.

Then he was in the thick of it again as a hooded figure came at him. Stepping to one side, Blake chopped him viciously behind the ear and the man went down with a sharp guttural sound, striking his head on the flagged floor.

It seemed that they had the upper hand. But even as the thought registered he saw Selman go down, blood pouring from his neck where it had been ripped open by a knife-blade. Thumbing a button on the bracelet, Blake spoke urgently into the tiny transmitter.

'Avon! It's Blake – get us up there!'

Avon and Jenna were transfixed as the speaker in the teleport section boomed out with Blake's terse command. And again, more insistently:

'Avon, get us up there! Make it fast!'

Jenna reached for the control and Avon grasped her wrist. His face was a stone mask.

'Touch that and we've lost it all.'

Her hand froze above the control, her eyes searching his.

Blake couldn't understand what had gone wrong. He spoke rapidly into the transmitter, his voice thin with a desperation he was fighting hard to control.

'*Avon! Jenna!* Do you hear me? We can't hold on here. Get us up –'

A blow on the side of the head sent him staggering. Blake shook his head dazedly in an effort to clear it and as he faced his attacker another hooded figure came at him, brandishing a knife. Blake twisted aside in the nick of time and felt the passage of air against his cheek as the man narrowly missed.

Without a weapon to defend himself, his chances were slim against two armed men. Arco saw his plight and came to help him, distracting the attention of one of the men; but he wasn't fast enough and received a gash in the shoulder, clinging on desperately as he sought to keep the knife from his throat.

By now Vargas had recovered. Circling round, he waited while Blake delivered a blow to his adversary's solar plexus, and in the next instant, as Blake's guard was momentarily relaxed, lunged at him, attacking from behind. Blake was sent sprawling, his wrist striking the floor so that the impact shook loose the bracelet and it went skittering into the shadows.

Blake tried to scramble after it, and as he did so Vargas stepped forward and kicked him savagely in the ribs. Blake collapsed, the wind knocked out of him, and stared helplessly as Vargas eased the handgun from its holster and with slow, calculating deliberation aimed the weapon directly at him. Vargas sneered arrogantly, enjoying his moment of triumph, and was about to press the button trigger when he vanished.

Into thin air.

As did Gan and Vila.

There was a moment of utter blank incredulity from the members of the faith, and it was just long enough for Blake to snatch up the bracelet, clamp it on to his wrist, and call into it:

'Avon, ship me up.'

In the teleport section there was a similar moment of confusion as Gan and Vila materialised. Jenna snapped at Avon, 'Order Zen to get the ship moving.'

Hiding his disappointment, Avon set off for the Flight Deck.

Jenna heard Blake's voice and operated the control, but she was totally unprepared as another figure materialised who looked about him in bewilderment, but then quickly recovered and raised his handgun threateningly.

'Move over there – all of you!' Vargas snarled, sizing up the situation.

As they obeyed, Blake materialised, but Vargas was quick to cover him.

'You'll take this ship down on to the surface,' he ordered.

'We're already moving away,' Jenna told him.

'Then turn it back.'

Blake said, 'Kill us and you'd have no way to run this ship – and remember, you're getting further and further away from your precious drug.'

Vargas snorted. 'Drug? There is no drug,' he said contemptuously. 'Chalk, that's all it was. And the disease a mild poison that soon clears.' The glint of madness entered his eyes. 'But for centuries the followers have *believed* in the disease, *believed* in the cure. Just as all of you *believed*!'

He laughed hoarsely, a strange demented cackle.

Blake nodded slowly, and with a barely perceptible flicker towards Jenna at the teleport control panel, moved to one side so that Vargas had to step back a pace to keep him covered. He was standing less than a metre outside the transmission area.

'So you – you and those before you – built your power on their fear,' Blake said flatly. 'You ruled them with it.'

'I ruled a small prison planet with never more than five hundred people. But with this – ' Vargas made a grand gesture which encompassed the *Liberator* ' – with this,

151

crewed by my followers, I could rule a thousand planets,' he gloated. 'For that prize do you think I would hesitate to kill any of you . . . all of you? Now turn the ship back to Cygnus Alpha. *Now.*'

Blake made as if to move forward again and Vargas edged backwards, eyeing him warily. He was now inside the transmission area.

'I was their priest,' Vargas crooned insanely, 'but I will return to them –'

Jenna punched the control.

'– a GOD!'

The shimmering light encapsulated him and he began to fragment, his mouth gaping as he uttered the final word, and as he disappeared into the void, his body disintegrating into billions of sub-atomic particles, the word seemed to echo after him in a long mournful wail.

Then he was gone, leaving only a silent emptiness.

Seated at the main flight control module with Jenna beside him, Blake was checking their position on the astro-navigation chart. Avon, Gan and Vila were busying themselves with various tasks, getting the feel of the ship's complex network of control systems.

A light flashed on the panel in front of him and Blake pressed a button to acknowledge it. He turned expectantly to the computer.

'*Hull sensors register that we have been scanned by detector beams,*' Zen informed them, the soft mechanical voice quite expressionless. '*Three ships at the edge of the galaxy have changed course and turned toward us.*'

'Put them on the screen,' Blake ordered curtly.

The large screen filled with the dense blue-blackness of space, the myriad stars like cold pinpoints of light, and everyone turned to look at it. Nothing moved in all that vast expanse, all was silent and still, but then Jenna pointed to the edge of the screen where three minute specks were moving in a steady arc.

'There they are! Three of them.'

'Can they be identified?' Blake asked the computer.

A sequence of lights flickered and changed on Zen's display panel before it answered, *'Extreme range makes positive identification impossible. Based on available data they would be classified as Federation Pursuit ships.'*

'Looking for us?' Jenna asked Blake, worriedly.

Blake sighed and nodded wearily. He spoke to the computer. 'Set a course to take us away from them. Maximum speed.'

'Course and speed confirmed,' Zen responded, and clicked off.

Avon continued to look at the three blips on the screen. His expression was depressed, almost resentful. 'With our speed we can probably lose them this time,' he said bleakly. 'But they'll go on looking, tracking us, pushing us. They'll never give up!' he finished on a note of despair.

'And nor will we,' Blake said quietly. He gazed at the screen for a moment and then looked round at his four companions, his face set and deadly serious. 'We're not going to keep running and hiding. When we learn to handle this ship properly we'll stop running. We'll be a combat ship – and from then on we'll be fighting back!'

10

The caesium timepiece mounted on the flight control module marked off the seconds with atomic precision. Standing at Jenna's shoulder, Blake counted them silently as the holographic digits ticked towards zero.

This was the first full-scale test of operating the *Liberator* under manual control and the atmosphere on the Flight Deck was tense, everyone waiting alertly, hands poised over their individual nests of controls, eyes glued to the banks of instrumentation. There was no margin for error. It was vital that all crew members adhere rigidly to the procedure, performing their tasks with speed, accuracy and absolute dependability.

The digital display registered zero and Blake rapped out his orders:

'Cut primaries. Reverse thrust. Negative anti-grav. Stabilise and trim to stationary. Compensate for star system's orbital draft and hold . . . '

The ship's hyper-propulsion unit began a slow and steady decline in power output as each crew member activated a control and the throbbing whine gradually faded away to a low pulsing murmur.

All main functions were displayed on the central flight panel – a complex array of instrumentation which was Jenna's prime responsibility – and Blake flashed a questioning glance at her. She scanned the panel and then looked towards him.

'All confirmed,' she acknowledged with a relieved smile.

'Good. I'll check it against autos.' He leaned across, stabbed a button, and spoke into the computer receptor panel. 'Confirm status.'

The sequence of lights changed, relays whirred, and Zen reported:

'The ship is stationary and stabilised in an anti-orbital posture.'

Everyone sat back and breathed easy. Blake gave a grin of satisfaction and looked round the Flight Deck. 'You handled that well,' he told them all, really pleased. 'We're getting the hang of flying the ship manually – but more important, we're coming together as a crew.'

There was a general sense of pride and mutual congratulation, though Avon's face betrayed a rather bored and weary cynicism. He said caustically, 'Spare us the morale-boosting pep-talk, Blake. The only object of the exercise was to see if we've shaken off the pursuit ships.'

Blake hid an amused smile and pressed the computer button.

'I want a three-sixty spherical survey. Scanners and etheric beam detectors set at maximum range. Register and report any space vehicles within the sphere. Put a visual survey on the screen.'

Everyone's attention was focused on the screen as the scanner moved across the starscape in a 360-degree sweep. The computer clicked and buzzed softly to itself as it checked the ship's network of sensors, and everyone waited anxiously for the final verdict. When it came the tension drained away and there was a mood of jubilation.

'Negative readout on all systems. There are no space vehicles operating within our detector range.'

'Then we've lost them!' Jenna whooped.

'I was starting to think those Federation Pursuit ships were a permanent fixture,' Vila admitted, making a pantomime of wiping his brow. His small dark eyes danced with irrepressible mischievousness.

'But now we know we can outrun them,' said Gan, his broad face creasing in a pleased grin.

'Don't get too complacent,' Blake warned. 'We're in the clear for the moment but they'll go on looking for us.'

'It shouldn't be too difficult to stay out of their way,' Avon countered. 'We have the whole Universe to hide in –'

'Except that we're not hiding.' Blake's tone was firm, quite determined. 'In two space days they'll know exactly where we are . . . or at least where we've been.'

They all watched him curiously and Vila asked what he meant by that.

'Until now we've been nothing more than a minor irritation. A scratch. It's time we turned that scratch into an open wound.' Blake's eyes were cold, unyielding. 'We're going to really hurt them.'

Jenna gave a mock groan. 'Oh no . . . I don't like the sound of this.'

'Wait a minute, Blake.' Avon sat up straight, his expression wary. 'I don't know what kind of wild scheme you've got in mind, but right at the outset you agreed that we wouldn't get into anything without first talking it through.'

'That's right,' Blake conceded amiably. 'I also said that any time anybody didn't like the way I was running this ship they can be put down and left on the nearest habitable planet.' He smiled and said lightly, 'Just tell me when you want to leave.'

Avon glanced round at the others. He cleared his throat and said after a moment, 'Well I – I just think we have a right to know what's happening . . .'

Blake nodded curtly and spoke to the computer.

'We're going into star system 4. Set course for the planet Saurian Major. Speed: time distort five.'

'*Speed and course confirmed,*' came the prompt response.

'Saurian Major,' Jenna frowned. 'I've heard of that.'

Blake called them to the main console and spread the astro-navigation chart so everyone could see. He pointed out the planet to them.

'It's right here on the edge of the system. It was colonised at the beginning of the second calendar. Annexed by the Federation two hundred years ago. Not too long back, the settlers declared it an independent planet. The Federation treated the claim as armed insurrection and put in a force of occupation. Half the population was wiped out and most of the others were transported to the outer systems for resettlement. The few that got away are still living in the hills. They fight as guerillas but they're under strength and under-armed –'

Vila changed feet impatiently. 'So cut the history lesson. Why are we going there? What makes it special?'

Blake looked round the circle of faces. 'Because it has a unique position in the galaxy. It makes a perfect communications relay centre. All Federation signals and space controls are beamed into Saurian Major, boosted and redirected. They've built a vast trans-receive complex . . . everything goes through there . . . it's a vital nerve in the Federation space control system. They hear, see and speak through it.' He paused, watching their absorbed, intent faces, and said firmly, 'Cut that nerve and you blind, deafen and silence them. That's what we're going to do!'

Vila whistled softly. Nobody else uttered a sound.

It was while Blake and Jenna were manning the Flight Deck that the unknown object first presented itself to them. More perplexed than concerned, Jenna studied the small green blipping glow on the long-range sonar display; it reappeared every time the scanner turned to forward projection. She observed it with growing puzzlement for some time before turning to Blake at the astro-navigation desk.

'Do the charts show any satellite paths intersecting our course?'

'I'll check.' But after a brief interval, he shook his head. 'Nothing marked. You getting a reading?'

'I'm not sure,' Jenna said slowly, trying to resolve the definition. 'Take a look at this.'

Blake came to stand beside her chair. He too watched the oscillating green light for several moments before asking, 'How long has it been showing?'

'A couple of minutes. It started as a very weak signal . . . much stronger now.'

'The same pattern?' he enquired.

'Yes.' Jenna looked up at him. 'What do you think?'

'It could be a call-sign,' Blake hazarded. 'But it's certain there's something ahead of us.'

'It can't be very large or it would show on the forward scan,' Jenna pointed out.

'We'll get a detector reading,' Blake decided, stepping across to the computer panel. He thumbed a button. 'Detectors. I want an electro-magnetic analysis on the signal on circuit eight.'

Zen's bank of indicator lights flashed briefly and steadied.

The signal is mechanical in origin. It emanates from a space projectile of unknown manufacture. Translator units categorise the signal as a distress call.

'Estimate projectile's speed and course.'

The sequence of lights changed, became static.

The projectile shows no indication of motive power,' Zen reported. *'Its movement is subject to space drift and orbital influence.'*

Jenna looked at Blake. 'If they've lost power they're in bad trouble. What are we going to do?'

'We don't have much choice.' Blake spoke to the computer. 'How far away are we?'

'One million seventy-three spacials and closing.'

Blake drummed his fingers on the console, considering

this, then said crisply, 'Reprogram speed and course to bring us alongside the projectile. Rendezvous and lock-on at a hundred spacials.'

'*Speed and course confirmed,*' came the bland reply.

'You'd better tell the others we're changing course,' Blake told Jenna, but she remained seated, small lines of concern on her forehead. 'What's the matter?' he asked her.

'It's just that . . . ' Jenna stared at him, biting her lip. 'Well, I think we should be more careful. Putting out a false distress signal is a trick used by space pirates. You come up alongside and they open up with their blasters.'

'There's always a risk,' Blake admitted. He shrugged slightly. 'But we can't just ignore the call.'

'I know, but let's take what precautions we can.' Jenna gave him a meaningful look and crossed to the inner door leading to the crew's quarters. 'I'll warn the others.'

As she went out Blake moved across to the sonar display and stood watching the green blip oscillating on a regular frequency; he continued to watch it, wondering what 'a space projectile of unknown manufacture' was doing in this quadrant of the galaxy. There had to be a reason, but Blake couldn't think of one.

Neither could Avon, when some time later he joined Blake on the Flight Deck and carried out an exhaustive multi-channel investigation which produced precisely nothing. Looking up from the communications console, he more or less conceded defeat.

'I've beamed in every type of signal,' Avon said, a note of exasperation in his voice. 'There's nothing coming back except the same distress call. It must be on a mechanical repeater.'

'It could be their receivers are out,' Blake suggested.

'Or there's nobody alive to read our signals . . . '

Zen interjected with, '*Slowing to halt and locking on to rendezvous position.*'

'Put it on the screen,' instructed Blake.

The two men turned to observe the panorama of stars which as the scanner revolved brought into view a small bullet-shaped craft drifting in the void. It was obviously built for very high speed flight, the smooth featureless hull tapering to a sharp nose-cone, and lacking the usual tail-fins and stabilisers necessary for close manoeuvring.

'You recognise the type?' Blake asked after they had studied the projectile for a minute or so.

'No.' Avon shook his head dubiously. 'I wouldn't have thought it was built on any of the Fed planets. Too primitive and too small to sustain a full life-support system.'

'It doesn't seem to be carrying weapons,' Blake noted.

'My guess is a high speed transporter,' Avon surmised. He sniffed. 'But to transport what?'

'Let's find out.'

Together they left the Flight Deck and headed for the teleport section where they found the others clustered round a small monitor screen, all of them it seemed, equally bemused by the mystery craft. Blake directed Avon to the teleport control panel and requested him to get a precise fix on it.

'You're not going across?' Vila said with some alarm.

'I can't think of any other way to find out what's on board,' Blake replied, taking a bracelet from the rack and snapping it on his wrist. As an afterthought he took another bracelet and held it out. 'Anybody coming with me?'

The response wasn't immediately enthusiastic, but then Jenna stepped forward, accepting his offer. 'Why not?' she shrugged. 'It'll do me good to get out and about a bit.'

Blake handed a gunbelt to her, strapping one on himself, and turned to the others. 'We'll keep the voice channel open, just in case. If we should lose contact or if we sound like we're in trouble, pull *Liberator* back to a safe distance.'

'And if you do have trouble?' Vila queried speculatively.

'Use your own judgement. But on no account hazard the

ship.' He looked over to Avon at the teleport control panel.
'You set?'

'Ready,' Avon affirmed, his hands poised above the controls.

Blake and Jenna took their places in the transmission area.

'Put us over.'

Almost at once the shimmering cocoon of light enveloped them and their bodies seemed to distort and fragment, as if seen through a wave of intense heat. When the glare faded they were gone.

Jenna hadn't known what to expect of her first experience of teleportation, but whatever expectations she might have had were confounded by the total absence of any appreciable sensation. It could almost have been classified as a non-event – except for the simple fact that it worked. One instant she was in the *Liberator*, the next in a dark cramped space with just enough room to stand upright. The interior of the craft was little more than a basic shell-like structure, with most of the space taken up by three long cylindrical containers, two of them built into the walls, the third in the centre, forming a narrow aisle on either side. The containers were linked to the walls and floor by heavy cables and several lengths of silver corrugated tubing. Fitted into the end of each container a light in a perspex bubble glowed steadily: two of them green, the third – in the right-hand wall – red.

In the nose of the projectile there was a simplified control panel with a single indicator light flashing continuously.

'Not exactly built for comfort, is it?' Jenna remarked, after a cursory examination. There were no seating arrangements, and the projectile was too small to contain facilities for a crew.

'Have you seen anything like it before?' Blake asked. He

had moved along the aisle to the rear of the craft where a sturdy-looking circular hatch gave access to a further compartment. He tried to open it but the hatch remained securely locked.

'No,' Jenna confessed, checking the crude instrument display. 'The controls are very basic. Just about enough instruments to make a safe landing. No automatics, all manual.'

Blake edged forward along the narrow aisle. 'Why would they put manual controls in an unmanned ship?' he puzzled.

Jenna shrugged and pointed to the flashing light. 'The distress relay, still putting out the signal. It probably cuts in automatically if a major fault develops.' She scanned the dials and snapped her fingers. 'Got it.'

'What?'

'Circuit tracer.' Jenna showed him. 'There's a malfunction reading on the auto-navs. It must have activated a cut-out on the propulsion units.'

Blake wasn't entirely satisfied. 'That explains part of it,' he agreed, 'but it still doesn't make sense. You don't build things like circuit tracers into unmanned craft. There must have been a crew on board.'

'Then where are they?' Jenna indicated a door in the hull. 'The inner locks are still secure, and something this small wouldn't carry life rockets.' She looked towards the hatch at the rear of the craft. 'What about the other door?'

'Locked on this side,' Blake told her, 'though I couldn't open it.'

'So if there was a crew,' Jenna conjectured slowly, 'they're still here . . .'

She caught Blake's eye and together they turned to survey the three pod-like containers in the body of the craft. Blake knelt down to examine the central container. Adjacent to the glowing green light was a small rectangular switchbox. Drawing his handgun from its holster, Blake pressed the lever down and the curved metallic top section of the container began to slide open, revealing the full length of the interior. It contained a man.

He was in a comatose condition, eyes shut, arms by his sides, sealed in a round thermoplastic cylinder. There was something about his face – a cruel, ruthless quality – that made Jenna shudder. His hair was cropped very close so that it fitted his skull like a cap.

She stared at him, fascinated, and then gasped, 'His eye! Look at his eye!'

A tiny regular pulse was beating at the corner of his right eye.

'He's alive!' Jenna exclaimed.

Blake bent nearer and his hand happened to touch the thermoplastic cover. He reacted sharply and pulled back as if burned.

'What is it?' Jenna asked tersely.

'Cold . . . ' Blake winced, rubbing his hand. 'It's taken the skin off my fingers.'

Then Jenna had a sudden realisation. She gripped Blake's arm.

'A cryogen capsule! That's it – it was a system tried out centuries ago. They used it on the early deep space probes. The crews were subjected to phenomenally low temperatures and the ageing processes were suspended. This must be the same thing.'

Blake moved across to one of the containers mounted in the bulkhead and activated the cover. A brief glance was enough to show that its occupant was in a similar state to the first. Jenna was examining the other container, whose light glowed red, and her startled gasp brought him scurrying over.

There was a crack in the thermoplastic shell and the man inside was only vaguely discernible through a heavy covering of ice crystals. It was impossible to tell if he was alive or dead.

Jenna shivered and quickly resealed him in his icy tomb.

163

'There's not much we can do for them here,' Blake concluded. 'It will be a long slow process to raise the temperature to reanimate.'

'But we can't just leave them,' Jenna objected.

Blake mulled the problem over and then spoke into the tiny transmitter on the teleport bracelet.

'Avon, do you read?'

'I hear you,' came the immediate reply.

'Let's see how good you are in handling the ship in precision flying.' Blake winked at Jenna, a twinkle of impish amusement in his eye, and went on briskly, 'Open the locks on the lower hold and manoeuvre around to take us on board.'

'It's too chancy, Blake.' There was a note of real alarm in Avon's voice. 'It will be like threading a needle in the dark. Come on, be sensible –'

'The crew here is alive,' Blake interrupted. 'We can't abandon them.'

'But if the *Liberator* so much as nudges that ship, if we're a fraction of a degree out, you could go into a spin that could crack you up and rip the bottom off *Liberator*.' Avon's concern was apparent even over the teleport link.

Blake was unmoved. 'Then you'd better get it right,' he replied calmly. 'Out.'

Jenna raised her eyes to the upper bulkhead and crossed the fingers on both hands. 'Slowly, Avon,' she besought him. 'Take it very slowly.'

Avon, Villa and Gan didn't hear her earnest prayer, but in any case it wasn't really necessary: all three were acutely aware of the risk involved and the critical hairline manoeuvring required to comply with Blake's request. Avon's initial reaction had been one of trepidation amounting almost to panic, but this quickly gave way to single-minded determination when he realised that as much as anything else this was a test of his skill under close space conditions.

Turning to the other two, he rapped out brusquely, 'All right, let's show him!'

They hurried up to the Flight Deck and took their positions, Avon assuming command of the operation at the central flight control console. He took a breath, braced himself, and gave his first order:

'Inner hatches air locked.'

Vila obeyed with swift practised movements, his usual lighthearted irreverence replaced by a confident professional dedication. 'Hatches locked,' he confirmed crisply.

'Equalise lower hold pressure,' Avon called to Gan.

'Confirmed.'

'Open main locks.'

Vila operated the control and there was a mounting whine of hydraulics as the lower stern section of the vessel began to open, dropping downwards to form a ramp. It resembled a huge hinged jaw, big enough to swallow a normal-sized spacecraft whole, and in comparison with the diminutive projectile it was like a whale about to gulp down a minnow.

'Stern ramp fully open,' Vila reported.

Avon wiped his mouth, nodding to Gan. This was the tricky part. 'Stern scanners on screen,' he instructed, and as the image appeared they could see the projectile about twenty metres below them, now directly nose on to the rear of the *Liberator*.

Now it was up to Avon, and no one could help him. He gingerly operated the flight controls with the touch of a man juggling with eggs.

'Moving round to line up,' he murmured, his eyes glued to the screen. 'Right lateral. Minimum power.'

The vast bulk of the *Liberator* swung slowly into position, the projectile gleaming dully like a bullet against the vivid backdrop of stars.

'Too much!' Vila cried out. 'We're overshooting!'

'Left lateral,' Avon responded evenly. 'That's enough. Hold it there.'

The projectile was now directly in line, facing the ramp.

'Square on,' Avon advised, undating his crew. 'Give me a four-line laser projection.' A grid of laser beams was superimposed on the screen, acting as a guide. 'All right, we're aligned and ready to back up. You all set?' he asked the others, and received answering nods. 'Here we go. Commencing reverse.'

Slowly, its movement almost imperceptible, the huge ship began to reverse on to the tiny projectile. Gradually the distance between them lessened until they were practically touching.

'That's nice,' Avon crooned softly. 'Gently now ... easy ... easy ... easy ...'

The projectile was almost up to the ramp.

'Switch scanner to lower hold viewers.'

The screen changed to show the sharp nose of the projectile as seen from within the hold itself, the upper bulk of the ship masking it in deep shadow.

'Good ... good ... dead in line ...'

Everything was going perfectly. Another few seconds and it should be –

'She's turning!' Vila cried frantically.

'Lateral right, fast!' Avon's voice was cold, almost brutal as he snapped out the command. On the screen he could see the projectile at an angle to the stern ramp. Hell's bells, he thought, if her alignment gets out of true and she goes into a spin ...

'She's drifting out of the laser projection!' Gan called out warningly.

'Take us down degree point oh-one,' Avon rapped.

'You're too close!' Vila almost leapt out of his chair, trying to attract Avon's attention. 'She's going to hit the ramp broadside on!'

'Get her around!' Gan pleaded.

Avon refused to be rushed into hasty action. 'Down another point. More lateral.'

The projectile was now almost broadside on to the stern ramp.

'You're going to hit her!' Vila yelled. 'Pull away, Avon!'

'No, we're coming round.' Avon remained calm, handling the controls delicately, and the screen confirmed that the angle had been reduced. 'Gan, when the nose is on the laser projection I'm giving her full reverse thrust . . . '

With agonising slowness the projectile's nose turned once again to point into the hold of the *Liberator*. Everyone waited with bated breath for what had to be the one and only moment.

It came.

'Now!' Gan barked.

Avon grasped the throttle control and pulled it forward with an abrupt, decisive movement. The huge ship responded instantly and backed on to the projectile swallowing it in a single swift gulp.

Vila let out a whoop of jubilation. 'You've done it! You've done it!' He beamed triumphantly, swinging round in his chair.

'Side scan,' Avon requested, making absolutely sure before relaxing his concentration. The screen showed a side view of the projectile in the hold.

'Well done,' Gan congratulated him.

'Terrific,' Vila added, brimming with elation. 'And you didn't even scratch the paintwork.'

Avon allowed himself a small grin of pride. 'Let's finish it off. Main locks close. Lower hold repressurised. Inner hatches released.'

When they had completed the final checks Avon deactivated the flight control panel and slumped back in his chair. He felt exhausted.

Vila came over and pounded him on the shoulder. 'That was as nice a piece of flying as ever I saw,' he declared enthusiastically. 'Come on, let's get down to the hold and see what we've caught.'

Avon roused himself and followed the small bouncing man across the Flight Deck.

The bulkhead globes threw a pale wash of light over the smooth streamlined shape of the projectile, resting in the centre of the cavernous interior of the rear hold. The small slim craft looked lost in the huge, echoing area; in fact it was little larger than one of the *Liberator*'s own survival pods.

Avon and Vila entered through the bulkhead door and hurried across the expanse of metalled flooring, just in time to hear the inner locks squealing in protest as they were manually released. The small hatch in the side of the craft slowly opened and first Jenna, then Blake, emerged, blinking a little as they stepped down.

'Welcome back,' chirped Vila, peering inquisitively inside the craft. 'What have we got here?'

'Take a look,' Blake invited. He patted Avon's shoulder and gave him an appreciative look. 'Well done.'

'I wish I were modest enough to say "it was nothing", but in fact it was a brilliant manoeuvre.' Avon gave a wry smile and hoisted himself after Vila through the hatch.

Blake strode across to a wall communicator and punched a button.

'Flight Deck,' Gan acknowledged.

'Blake. Have Zen resume course for Saurian Major. Speed: time distort five.'

'Confirmed.'

Jenna was examining the exterior of the hull. The surface was scarred and pitted, seared by cosmic radiation, and there was a row of faded symbols she was trying to decipher.

'Make anything of it?' Blake asked her.

Jenna shook her head. 'Most of it's been scraped away. It's Earth style lettering, all right, but a very old form.'

'From the condition of the hull it must have been in space for a long time. Look at that meteorite scarring.'

'Any idea where it might have come from?'

Blake contemplated the chipped and flaking craft and then suggested, 'It might be more interesting to know where it was going and why. Let's see what Avon can make of it.'

He hauled himself up through the hatch and worked his way along one of the narrow aisles into the nose section. Avon and Vila had opened the covers on the cylindrical containers and were gazing at the occupants inside their sealed cryogenic environment.

'What do you think?' Blake asked them.

Avon looked around and then shrugged. 'I could give you a few guesses. The ship's pretty old, or from a culture that hasn't developed very far in space travel. She's sub-lightspeed, so her destination must have been out of the star system in which she was launched.'

Vila frowned quizzically. 'How do you work that out?'

'It's obvious.' Avon gestured towards the three containers. 'The only reason they'd put the crew into suspended animation is because the journey would take longer than the natural lifespan of a man. The cryo system would halt ageing and decay. These three – ' he checked himself and amended ' – these two, rather, could be hundreds of years old. And a couple of other things seem fairly clear. Their destination was a civilised planet.'

'Why do you say that?' Blake asked sharply.

Avon swept his hands to indicate the bleak interior. 'Look at the equipment. There are none of the instruments or devices that you'd need to make an exploratory landing on an unknown planet.' He shook his head emphatically. 'No, I'd say this was a straightforward shuttle designed to carry three people to a known destination.'

'That makes sense,' Blake conceded thoughtfully.

'You want one more guess?'

'Go ahead.'

'The ship is not armed. No sign of any weapons in here

. . . so they were going somewhere where they knew they'd have a friendly reception.'

Vila made a disgruntled face. 'Well,' he muttered sourly, 'I hope you are one hundred per cent wrong!'

'Why?' Avon blinked, slightly put out.

'Because there's nothing worse than a know-it-all who also happens to be right!' Vila asserted comically.

'Well, we should know for certain pretty soon,' Avon remarked. 'I've cut in the reanimate circuit. It'll take a while but these two should resume normal life-cycle. Then they can tell us what they're all about.'

'Anything we can do to speed up the process?' Blake enquired.

Avon shook his head. 'No, it's all programmed. Interfere with it and you might kill them.'

'All right.' Blake stretched himself wearily and yawned. 'No point in waiting around. We'll take a look at them in a couple of hours.'

He motioned Vila to precede him and all three edged awkwardly towards the hatch, keeping their heads low. As they were about to climb out Avon noticed the door at the rear of the compartment.

'Did you take a look in there?'

'No. I tried but it was locked.'

Avon gave it a brief appraisal and said casually, 'Probably the navigation and power systems.'

They stepped down into the hold where Jenna awaited them. Together all four started for the bulkhead door when Avon had a sudden thought. 'There is something we could do,' he notified Blake, halting. 'Take out the program and auto-nav box. We could link it in to the computer and get a reading on the planet of origin and the projectile's course and destination.'

Blake agreed it was worth a try.

'Leave it to me, I'll get it,' Jenna said promptly, and as

170

the three men went on she turned back and clambered in through the hatch.

Kneeling down in front of the control panel, she removed the retaining clips which held the cover in place and slid it to one side. The maze of solid-state control equipment was ancient, but all the primary circuits were plainly marked and she had no difficulty in tracing the multi-coloured leads to the small black box which housed the auto-nav and its pre-set program tape. It was a fiddly job, disconnecting the transducers and unfastening the tiny copper screws, and she became quite absorbed in the task.

The three containers lay open behind her. In the central one, connected to the floor by the corrugated tubes, the body of the man with close-cropped hair lay stiffly like a wax effigy. He might have been dead – and a casual glance would have confirmed this impression – but as Jenna worked, silently absorbed, the fingers of his left hand started to twitch, and the hand itself was beginning to flex very, very slightly.

11

'You getting anywhere with that?'

Blake stood at Avon's elbow and watched as he connected the auto-nav box to the computer terminals and after a moment's cogitation began tapping in instructions on the keyboard.

'Not yet.' Avon paused and jotted down a rough calculation on a scrap of paper. 'The decoders haven't figured out the notational system yet. It might take a while,' he advised.

Blake looked round the Flight Deck. 'Has anybody been down to check on them lately?' he asked the others.

'Vila went down a little while ago,' Jenna replied, glancing up.

'How are they coming?'

Vila waggled his ears. 'Defrosting nicely,' he reported with a grin. 'Couple of hours and we should be able to talk to them.'

Zen's indicator lights began to flash and Blake stepped quickly across and touched the audio control.

'*We are in the approach zone of the planet Saurian Major. Slowing to stop and assuming a fixed orbit one thousand spacials from the surface.*'

Blake spoke into the receptor panel. 'Hold position until further orders.' He straightened up, suddenly alert, and his voice became brisk and businesslike. 'Avon, Vila, get ready.

You two are coming with me. Jenna, you stay aboard with Gan. I want one of you standing by at all times. We may need to get off Saurian quickly.'

'Right,' Jenna responded crisply.

Everyone started to move.

In the teleport section, Vila handed out weapons and equipment while Jenna settled in position at the control desk. Blake took several bracelets from the rack, gave one each to Avon and Vila, clipped on his own, and zipped a number of spares into an arm pouch. Turning to Jenna, he issued explicit instructions:

'Put Zen on to constant scan. I want to know right away if those Federation Pursuit ships move into this system. Keep the voice channel open – we'll call in at regular intervals.'

'How long are you staying down?'

'I don't know,' Blake said frankly. 'Depends on what we find.' He checked his chronometer. 'A Saurian day is about thirty-six Earth hours. That should be all the time we need.' He held up his crossed fingers and grinned at her, though she sensed that his jocular manner belied the real danger and serious purpose of the mission they were about to undertake.

'You all set?' Blake asked his two companions.

Avon and Vila nodded and all three entered the transmission area.

'Right,' Blake ordered. 'Put us down.'

Everything was red: the sky, the terrain, the vegetation, even the air they breathed. Vila was alarmed. He looked down at his hands and saw that they too were red and gulped audibly. Had he landed in a nightmare belonging to someone else? Fortunately for his sanity Blake and Avon were in the nightmare with him – admittedly with a reddish tinge.

'What is it?' he asked, staring about him. 'Is it something in the atmosphere?'

Blake was getting his bearings. 'Yes,' he answered off-handedly. 'There's an upper layer gas strata that filters out the other parts of the spectrum and gives everything a reddish hue. You'll get used to it.'

They were in a small clearing scattered with boulders, and there was something else that Vila found disturbing – the strange vegetation. He couldn't think what it was, but there was a certain quality about it that made the hairs on his spine prickle. He reached out and touched a waving frond and yelped in digust. The feel of it was loathsome.

'Did it sting you?' Avon asked.

'No . . . ' Vila shuddered. 'It's warm . . . sort of clammy.' He swallowed and his voice came out in a shrill squeak. 'Like flesh.'

Blake was scanning the horizon. 'You have to be careful with the plant life here. There are some species with an intelligence rating.' He glanced over his shoulder at them. 'And some of them are carnivorous.'

'Oh that's nice,' Vila reassured himself cheerfully. 'I can have a cosy chat with a plant while it's eating me.' He glowered melodramatically at the gently waving frond.

Blake had taken a map from his pocket and they gathered round while he indicated their position.

'The teleport put us down here.' His finger traced a route to the north. 'And the communications complex is here.'

'How do you intend to make contact with the rebels?' Avon wanted to know.

'I don't.' Blake folded the map and put it away. 'With a bit of luck they'll contact us. We won't make any secret about being here. We'll set up camp and light a fire.'

Vila looked round as if someone might be skulking in the undergrowth. 'And if the security forces see us first?' he enquired nervously.

'That's a chance we have to take.' Blake gathered up a handful of twigs and dry grass. 'Come on, let's get started.'

*

Gan had lowered his chair to a semi-reclining posture and was leaning back, staring placidly into space. Jenna didn't know how he could remain so calm; nothing ever seemed to upset the big man. He always seemed so content, never allowing anything to ruffle his calm exterior and philosophical attitude to life.

She herself felt restless, wandering aimlessly round the Flight Deck, checking the black box wired-in to the computer and then glancing at the screen which showed the continuous spherical scan of the Saurian Major system. Finally she settled down in a chair. The ship seemed very quiet, the silence pressing heavily.

'We've still got an empty sky,' she remarked at length. 'No sign of Pursuit ships.'

Gan stirred. 'They'll find us, sooner or later.' His voice was resigned, as if stating an obvious and unavoidable fact.

'I keep wondering if it wouldn't be better to opt out of all this,' Jenna said morosely, her slender fingers feeling the texture on the thickly padded arm. 'Find a nice safe planet and stay there.'

'They'd find you.'

Jenna nodded bleakly. 'I suppose.'

'But if you did want to leave, Blake wouldn't try to stop you.'

'I know.' She looked across at the heavily muscled man, studying him for a moment. 'What about you, are you going to stick with him?'

'I have to,' Gan stated quietly. 'I want to stay alive and to do that I need a few people I can count on.' He gazed unseeingly at the large screen. 'I can't be on my own.'

Jenna's eyes clouded in puzzlement. 'I don't understand.'

'If it ever comes to kill or be killed, I can't win on my own.' Gan leaned forward and parted his hair so that Jenna could see the small bald patch with its criss-crossed pattern of stitching scars.

'An implant?'

Gan nodded and sat back. 'A limiter. I can defend myself up to a point but the limiter makes me incapable of killing.'

'Even if you were going to be killed yourself?' she asked him, perturbed by the notion.

'That's what I meant when I said I need people I can count on. If it came to the crunch – ' he held out his hand and tightened it into a meaty fist ' – I'd just lock, mentally and physically. I'm incapable of directly causing the death of another.'

'Was the implantation ordered by the Court?'

'No, it was done before my trial,' Gan replied blandly, and went on as if he were recounting an incident that had happened to someone else. 'They needed humans for their research, so I was just handed over. Most of the time it has no effect, only if I'm involved in a situation where there is violence or aggression. That's when it operates.'

'I suppose it would be no bad thing if we all had implants,' Jenna said ruminatively. 'I'm surprised the Federation haven't thought of applying it on a massive scale.'

'I think they have,' Gan told her. 'But if you have a total population unable to kill, where do you recruit your armies? What do you do when you're faced with attack by races who don't have limiters?'

'You mean it would have to be universal?'

Gan spread his hands. 'And even if it were implanted in every child at birth a few might get through the net.' He had obviously thought it through. 'A small handful who were ruthless enough could control everything. And don't doubt it . . . there were groups in government who would like to achieve that.'

Jenna considered this and the far-reaching implications it would have; nothing was ever as simple as it seemed. She found it depressing, for it meant that wars were an inevitable and inescapable fact of existence for all supposedly intelligent life-forms throughout the Universe.

'Time we went down and had a look at our guests,' Gan proposed, elevating his chair to the upright.

Jenna stood up quickly, feeling the need to do something rather than just sit around waiting. 'Don't bother, I'll go. You keep an eye on the scanner.'

She flashed him a brief smile and headed for the inner door. Within a few minutes she had descended to the lower level and spun the locking wheel on the bulkhead door which gave access to the rear hold. Stepping through she was immediately struck by the silent vastness of the place, like the shadowy interior of one of the old aircraft hangars she had seen holograph prints of in the history books. The metalled flooring gleamed in dull streaks from the wall globes, and the projectile, its hull pitted and scarred from the battering of space debris, seemed almost like an ominous presence amidst the silence and deep shadow.

Jenna moved towards it, trying to ignore the vague sense of unease that plagued her. Pausing near the open hatch she heard the slow steady drip of water, and looking down noticed that a small pool had formed on the floor immediately below.

Glancing round, she couldn't rid herself of the feeling that she was being observed, but then with an annoyed shrug of her shoulders dismissed the idea and climbed up into the projectile. The cramped, gloomy interior contained a faint yet distinctly unpleasant smell, and it took her a moment to register its source. It came from the right-hand container, and she started involuntarily at the sight of the figure that lay inside, which previously had been covered with ice. The man could now clearly be seen, his face ravaged by aeons of time, his gaunt shrunken cheeks flaking away and the skull almost showing through the rotting flesh. Long matted grey hair adhered tenuously to his scalp and a fallen strand obscured his sightless eyes.

Jenna shook herself and slid the cover down to hide the disgusting sight. She turned to inspect the other two and frowned when she saw that the covers were closed . . . surely they had been left open? Kneeling by the central container, she slid the cover open and looked at the man inside the thermoplastic capsule. The area round his head was misted. Cautiously she attempted to lift the curved inner seal, and after a momentary resistance it slid back and she was able to view him properly.

In his early thirties, she guessed, though it was difficult to be absolutely sure because the harsh lines of his face and close-cropped hair gave him a severe, curiously ageless appearance. He was now breathing slowly and rhythmically, his chest rising and falling with each shallow breath, though his eyes remained shut. Taking his limp arm, Jenna felt for the man's pulse, and began counting silently.

Her heart lurched in her chest as abruptly, without any warning, his fingers suddenly snapped round her wrist like a steel trap and she was held fast in his fierce grip. His eyes, however, were still closed, and his breathing continued its steady regular rhythm.

Jenna let go a deep sigh of relief and prised her wrist free, the man's arm dropping limply by his side. Her heart was hammering from the shock and it took a moment or two to regain her composure, massaging her tingling wrist while she gazed at him in puzzled consternation. Where had he come from? How long had he been travelling through space? And what mysterious mission had he and his two companions been engaged upon? There was something odd about all this that perplexed and worried her.

Biting her lip, still completely baffled, she turned to the third container and slid the cover aside. For a blank split-second she couldn't believe the evidence of her own eyes.

The container was empty.

Getting swiftly to her feet, Jenna stumbled to the hatch and stared out apprehensively into the cavernous hold, the banks of deep shadow in the further corners now taking on a menacing aspect that made her throat constrict. He was

178

out there somewhere, hiding in the darkness, waiting for ...
what?

She glanced nervously back inside the craft and then had
a sudden thought. Moving slowly to the rear of the compartment she tried the solid-looking door. Still locked. That
clinched it. He had to be out there, concealed in the shadows.
God knew what was going through his mind after so many
years sealed at sub-zero temperatures in a cryogenic capsule.

Summoning up all her courage, Jenna stepped cautiously
down into the hold, her eyes flitting anxiously to the murky
recesses where she now knew for certain that someone was
watching. Her instinct had been right after all.

The man who still remained in the container had observed
her slim figure framed in the hatch. He remained perfectly
motionless, his head slightly raised, staring after her, eyes
narrowed, unblinking, fixated.

Meanwhile, Jenna had moved unhurriedly towards the
bulkhead door, not wishing to alarm the hidden watcher in
the shadows. In the middle of the floor she paused and
swivelled slowly round. She took a deep steadying breath
and called out in what she hoped was a reasonably firm
voice:

'I know you're here. There's no need to hide. We mean
you no harm. We want to help you ...'

The words echoed back hollowly from the gloomy depths
of the hold. She waited a moment and then tried again:

'We want to help you. Do you understand what I'm saying? Do you understand my language?'

Only her words came back, mocking her emptily.

There was the blur of an object, something glinted dully
in mid-air, and she was struck viciously on the right arm by
something hard and heavy which clattered to the metalled
floor. A large spanner lay at her feet, thrown accurately and
with considerable force. Gritting her teeth with pain, Jenna
swung round and gazed wildly in the direction the spanner

179

must have come from. Nothing stirred. Nursing her injured arm and keeping her eyes on the shadowed area, she backed slowly towards the nearest wall, then reached up gratefully with her left hand and unhooked the communicator.

The words flooded out in a panic of fear and terror.

'Gan! One of them is down here . . . he's hiding!'

There was no reply. The line sounded dead in her ears.

'Gan!' Jenna yelled frantically. 'Gan!'

She tore her eyes away from the menacing darkness and risked a glance at the cable leading to the communicator. It had been wrenched from the wall and severed with brute strength.

The air seemed to go solid and she couldn't get her breath. The fear was crawling up inside her, making the muscles of her stomach contract in a taut hard knot. Her legs were like jelly. Forcing herself to move, Jenna edged along the wall to the bulkhead door, which still stood open. She was trying to think coolly, rationally, but her thoughts were like snowflakes in a storm, whirling frenziedly, and it was as if the surrounding darkness was closing in on her, the shadows reaching out to engulf her.

She had almost reached the door – it was less than three metres away – when the muffled slap of a shoe on metal made her spin round and she saw a man bounding towards her, his face creased and ugly with murderous rage. His huge pale hands were fixed like claws in front of him, tearing his way towards her. Staggering backwards, Jenna fell through the open doorway, dragging the door shut behind her, but not quickly enough.

The man had gripped the edge of the door and was trying to heave it open. Jenna pulled with all her might but her right arm was still numb from the injury and she was fighting a losing battle. The gap slowly widened as the man exerted his superior strength, Jenna clinging on desperately, her feet slithering forward as the door inched open.

Having gained this advantage, the man snaked his arm

through the gap and sought to get a grip on her. His huge square hand swung near her face and Jenna, knowing it was her only chance, made a sudden lunging movement and buried her teeth in his wrist. The man cried out hoarsely and whipped his arm out of sight, leaving only one hand gripping the edge of the door, and with her last shreds of strength Jenna wrenched the door shut so that his fingers were smashed against the metal frame.

There was a further guttural cry of pain and the fingers were released.

Pulling the door fully shut, Jenna spun the locking wheel and then sagged weakly with heartfelt relief, supporting herself against the bulkhead and struggling to catch her breath.

She didn't delay long, and speedily made her way back to the Flight Deck, bursting in with the news already on her lips. 'Gan, one of them tried –'

She stared round in horrified disbelief. The Flight Deck was deserted.

'Gan!' Jenna shrieked, almost beside herself with wild-eyed terror.

And then, mercifully, he was there, emerging from an inner door.

'What is it?' he demanded, striding towards her, his eyes full of concern. 'What's happened?'

Jenna collapsed against him, sobbing with relief. 'One of them attacked me,' she told him breathlessly. 'I tried talking to him . . . but I couldn't get through . . . he came after me . . .'

'All right now, calm down,' he murmured soothingly. 'You're safe now, you're all right. Easy . . .'

He held her in his broad arm and led her to a chair. Jenna sank down, regaining control, breathing deeply.

'That's better,' Gan comforted her. 'Where is he now?'

'Still in the hold. I've locked the door.' She looked up at him anxiously. 'He was hiding, then he threw a wrench and practically broke my arm.'

'Let's take a look at it.'

Gan helped remove her jacket and shook his head at the sight of the dark bruise welling on her upper arm.

'I tried to call you but the cable on the communicator was torn out,' Jenna went on. 'Then he rushed at me –'

'He was probably just as frightened as you were,' Gan grunted. He went across to a locker and took out a medical kit.

'Don't bet on it,' Jenna retorted. 'I was scared out of my mind.'

'He's been dead for . . . well, perhaps centuries,' Gan reminded her. 'Then he comes to life in a strange environment. He has no idea if you're friend or foe. In the same circumstances we might act the same way.'

Jenna nodded reluctantly. 'I suppose so.' She was calmer now. 'And we don't really know what kind of mental damage might have been done by long-term cryo-suspension. It might take the mind a whole lot longer than the body to readjust.'

'That's right.' Gan had taken a small oval-shaped device from the kit, which had a series of controls and dials along the top and a concave padded surface underneath. He applied it gently to the bruised area and the device emitted a low-frequency pulse and began to vibrate. This was an infra-sonic healer, which could penetrate through living tissue, and when he removed it a few moments later no trace of the bruise remained.

Jenna smiled her thanks and slipped back into her jacket.

Gan returned the medical kit to the locker and took down a gunbelt. 'You stay here,' he instructed, strapping it on. 'I'll go down and see if I can talk to him.'

'What's the good of that?' Jenna asked, indicating the handgun. 'You can't use it.'

'But he doesn't know that,' Gan responded with a crafty grin. 'Just pointing it can be very convincing.'

He set off for the door.

'Be careful,' Jenna warned.

'Don't worry,' Gan replied, and went out.

Jenna leaned back in the chair, feeling slightly more relaxed, and a subdued beep from the control desk alerted her. She pressed a button.

'Jenna.'

'Blake. We haven't made contact with any rebel groups so far. We're moving to chart reference three-three-four. We'll call in on arrival.'

'Confirmed.'

'Anything happening with the crew of the projectile?'

'One of them – ' Jenna began, and then thought twice about bothering Blake with the matter. He had enough on his hands as it was. 'They're recovering,' she amended smoothly. 'Everything is under control.' Hoping that this wasn't mere wishful thinking on her part.

'I'll check with you later.' Blake broke the connection on the teleport communicator and glanced round the small clearing. The smoke from the dying campfire rose straight up in a gently eddying spiral. He was disappointed that there hadn't been any response to his signal and was becoming apprehensive in case the security forces had spotted it.

Taking a compact two-way radio from his belt, he thumbed the transmit button and spoke into the mouthpiece.

'Blake. Have either of you found anything?'

There was a short burst of static followed by the tinny sound of Avon's voice. 'Not a thing.'

Then Vila reported, 'Nothing in my sector.'

'All right, move back up here and we'll try a new location. Out.'

He clipped the radio on to his belt, stooped down and was about to throw a handful of sand over the fire when he suddenly tensed. It might have been a noise or something

183

less definable – just the sense of a presence behind him – but Blake knew he was not alone. Casually shifting position, he moved to the other side of the fire, and still crouching stared intently into the bushes. A branch seemed to bend with unnatural movement, as if concealing someone, and Blake rose slowly to his feet, his hand reaching stealthily for his sidearm.

From behind a hand chopped down on the back of his neck. Blake fell awkwardly, twisting round, and a boot swung into his chest sending him backwards into the fire. Rolling out of the flames, he fumbled at his holster and the boot came down hard on his wrist and the next instant he was staring into the muzzle of a large, antiquated machine-gun. Its barrel was highly polished and the weapon had evidently been well cared for.

Partially dazed, Blake shook his head and stared up. His assailant was tall, slim, athletically supple – and she was incredibly beautiful into the bargain. But the most fascinating feature about her was the colour of her eyes. Blake had never in his life seen anything like them, nor anyone like her, and neither could he fathom out why a young, stunningly-attractive girl should be wearing camouflaged combat gear: military-style shirt and trousers and snug, tightly-laced jungle boots.

Surprises weren't over for the day. Someone spoke inside his mind. It was a hard, brusque voice, yet distinctly female, and it asked sharply, *Who are you?*

Blake looked round groggily. There was no one else in the clearing.

Answer my question!

'Was it you that spoke?' Blake asked in amazement. The girl was looking down on him, her mouth a hard firm line, her peculiar eyes quite cold and unflinching.

I telepathed, said the voice in his head. *I'm asking you for the last time – who are you?*

'Do you mind if I get up?' Blake muttered, struggling to

184

rise. Apparently she did mind, for a boot landed squarely in his chest, knocking him flat.

Move again before I tell you and I'll blow your head off, the voice told him harshly. *Now, what are you doing here?*

Blake slumped back. He seemed resigned to his fate. 'My name is Blake,' he answered submissively. 'I came here with two men. We're trying to make contact with a resistance group – '

How did you get here?

Blake raised his arm to point and instinctively the girl looked in that direction. Thrusting his leg straight out, Blake hooked his foot behind her left ankle and with a swift savage movement jerked the girl off her feet. As she went down he grabbed the muzzle of the machine-gun and rammed the butt into her stomach, then wrenched it from her grasp and swung it round to cover her. The girl lay panting at his feet, her face uncommonly pale, her eyes blazing with anger.

'Damn you!' she spat at him.

'So you *can* talk,' Blake said with grim satisfaction. 'Good, because there are some things I need to know.'

'I'll tell you nothing!' the girl snarled defiantly, raising herself up on her elbows and glowering at him.

'I'm not with the Federation Security Force,' Blake reassured her, keeping his voice calm and reasonable.

'I don't believe you.'

'I came here with two of my crew. We only arrived a few hours ago.'

'That's a lie!' the girl flung at him, curling her lip. 'I keep a check on the space port. Nothing has landed or gone out in months.'

Blake studied her for a moment, wondering how much he should reveal. The truth was that he had no real alternative but to trust her: he needed information and he needed it quickly. He explained patiently:

'Our ship doesn't need to land. We teleport down to the surface. It's pretty obvious that you're with the resistance fighters . . . or at least you know where they are.'

'What resistance fighters?' the girl asked sullenly. 'I don't know what you're talking about.' Her flashing eyes watched him suspiciously.

Blake sighed and went on doggedly, 'Look. We came here to make a strike against the Communications Centre. But to do that we need help. We need local knowledge –'

'Then you'll have to look for it somewhere else.'

The girl was obdurate and Blake gave it up as a lost cause.

'All right, fine,' he said shortly, nodding briskly, out of patience. 'I'll make contact some other way.' He tossed the gun disdainfully at her feet. 'Take it and get out of here. We'll manage without you.'

Purposely turning his back on her he began to gather his equipment together. The girl got to her feet, cradling the machine-gun in the crook of her arm, her face clouded with uncertainty. She backed away a few steps, making as if to turn and run, and then hesitated. Still keeping the weapon trained on him, she asked cautiously:

'Can you prove what you say?'

Blake went on with what he was doing, all but ignoring her. 'If I can get inside the centre I'll prove it with the biggest damned explosion you ever saw.'

The girl relented a little. 'I might be able to help you,' she admitted warily, not yet certain what to make of him. 'I'm not saying I can, I might . . . '

Blake turned towards her, his expression one of long-suffering stoicism. 'Well make up your mind. I don't have time to play games.'

She observed him for a moment longer, still not entirely convinced, and asked slowly, 'What is it you want to know?'

'Let's start with who you are,' Blake demanded curtly.

'Cally.' She fixed him with her large eyes. 'My name is Cally.'

Then swinging round in an incredibly fast arc she dropped

186

to one knee and levelled the machine-gun at the bushes on the far side of the clearing. Blake jerked back a pace, taken completely by surprise by the startling swiftness of her movement.

'Come out of there!' Cally ordered sternly.

The bushes quivered and then parted and a rather shame-faced Vila stepped into the clearing, his hands held up to show that he carried no weapon.

'Now that's what I call sharp, really sharp.' He gave a grin of grudging admiration. 'I didn't even move a muscle.'

'Is he with you?' Cally asked Blake.

'Yes.'

'So am I.'

All three spun round to see Avon standing behind a low rock, his handgun drawn and ready to fire.

'And I don't think she's all that good,' he remarked lightly, coming forward. 'I've had a gun on you the whole time.'

Cally glared at him, then shouldered the machine-gun with an abrupt derisive motion that more than adequately conveyed her feeling.

Blake faced the three of them. 'All right, now we've all established our credentials, let's get down to why we're here.'

'What's the hurry?' Avon enquired casually, appraising the tall slim girl whose femininity seemed enhanced rather than disguised by her combat outfit. 'I'd like to know more about this telepathic creature you've got here. Did you *learn* to do that?' he asked, intensely curious.

'No.' Cally seemed reluctant to say more, but then went on, 'I'm from the planet Auron. Telepathy is normal for the people on my planet, that's how we communicate. Other races seem able to receive telepathic messages but they can't transmit back.'

'You mean I can *hear* what you're thinking?' Vila asked, goggling at her.

'Only if I want you to.'

187

'Fascinating,' Avon murmured, shaking his head in genuine wonder.

'But disconcerting,' Blake concluded dryly. 'Look, as far as I'm concerned you can hold a seminar on telepathy when we've finished what we came here for.' He was anxious to complete the mission and get back to the safety of the ship. And with the girl to help them there was a better than average chance of success. 'How do we contact the resistance force?' he asked bluntly.

'There isn't a resistance.' Cally gazed at him. She spoke calmly, without emotion, stating facts. 'They're all dead.'

'What?'

'We were quite powerful and getting stronger all the time,' Cally went on in the same even tone. 'I was in communications. Essential work because the security forces were always trying to hunt us down, but they had no chance. We knew the hills and jungles too well. About six cycles ago we attacked the main generating plant and did a lot of damage . . . really hurt them. Then the reprisals wiped everybody out.'

'What happened?' Avon asked quietly.

'They released a short-life virus,' she said stonily. 'The plague took all humanoid life within days. The virus died off and that was that . . . '

'And you're the only survivor?' Vila said, aghast.

Cally nodded, then made a slight shrugging motion. 'Perhaps coming from another planet I had a natural immunity. I was sick like the rest of them but I came through it.'

'And you've been working alone ever since?' Blake asked her.

'Yes.' Cally's eyes were cold, dead inside. 'What I've been planning is to get into the complex and do as much damage as I can before they stop me.'

'You'd never get out alive,' Avon warned her dourly.

Cally's smile was empty, totally without humour. 'I should have died with the others. My death was delayed by a freak.

188

There's no point in putting it off any longer.'

'Then we're all after the same thing,' Blake declared firmly, 'only I didn't plan this as a suicide mission.' He faced her, his voice low and terse, wanting more than anything to convince this young, lovely girl that her life still had purpose, meant something. 'Look, you know the layout of the Communications Centre. Come with us and help us to get inside. That way we stand a chance of doing the maximum damage and getting out safely.'

The three men waited for her answer. Cally's vivid gaze seemed to drift away for a while, as if in contemplation of old friends and distant days. Then without a movement or emotion disturbing her beautiful, flawless face, she telepathed directly to Blake *I'll show you the way.*

Turning, she strode lithely across the clearing. Blake grinned at his two puzzled companions, scooping up his equipment and following her. 'We're on our way,' he informed them, leaving Avon and Vila exchanging blank looks and scrambling to catch up.

12

Jenna kept telling herself that there was nothing to worry about, but even so she was like a butterfly hovering over broken glass, unable to settle. Surely Gan should have returned by now? But when she glanced at her wrist chronometer, not too long a time had elapsed, and she castigated herself for being too impatient, too nervous, letting her imagination get the better of her. Besides, Gan was big enough to look after himself, wasn't he? Of course he was.

And yet the jittery unease wouldn't go away. She paced across the Flight Deck and on an impulse stopped to check that the computer terminals were still connected to the small black auto-nav box. No reason why they shouldn't be, she reprimanded herself sourly. Leaning across, she punched the button and spoke into the receptor panel.

'Have the computers decoded the projectile's log yet?'

Zen flashed its cryptic sequence of coloured lights and reported:

'The electronic notation has been deciphered. The translator units are converting into Earth linguistics. A full translation will be available shortly.'

Jenna nodded, straightening up, and as she did so all the lighting dimmed and then brightened again. What could have caused that? She looked around the deserted Flight Deck, hating its silence, praying for Gan to return quickly.

The lighting faded once again, remained dim for several seconds, and then resumed its normal glow.

Jenna punched the button and asked the Zen for an explanation.

'*Auto maintenance reports major energy drain on primary power circuits. Locators indicate loss occurring from link unit four in lower stern hold.*'

'I'd better check it out,' Jenna murmured to herself, and went rapidly towards the inner door, halting nervously as yet again the lights went dim, this time for a longer period before slowly brightening. The waiting and the silence, and now the recurring darkness, had begun to oppress her; what had been a vast, complex, brightly-lit spacecraft – a marvel of super-advanced technological achievement – now took on a sinister aspect, with its labyrinth of empty corridors, the many levels with their endless rooms filled with equipment and instrumentation, and beneath it all the vast silent lower holds, like the bowels of some gigantic prehistoric creature.

She walked slowly along the corridor, her vinyl-soled shoes making no sound, becoming more apprehensive with each passing moment. It suddenly occurred to her that she shouldn't have left the Flight Deck unattended – Gan had left her on watch – and Jenna hesitated, turned about, then halted again, in an agony of indecision. She felt totally alone, helpless, as if dark, inexplicable forces were crowding in around her and she was incapable of rational thought or positive action.

Think it through, she told herself calmly. Think logically and act decisively. Taking a breath, she turned back and headed for the teleport section. As she entered, the lighting dimmed, making pools of shadow behind the banks of instrumentation, and what had been a bright, cheerful place was transformed into a dark and menacing chamber. Hurrying across to the control panel, she unhooked the communicator and pressed the ALL STATIONS button, speaking softly and urgently into the mouthpiece.

'Gan . . . are you all right?'

Her breathless voice filled the ship, so that it sounded in her ears like an enormous whispering gallery, the words endlessly repeated in rooms and corridors, echoing back to her in a kind of mocking chorus.

Jenna held the communicator close to her mouth, her hand gripping it tightly, trying to control the fluttering panic that was rising like nausea in her chest.

'Gan . . . please call in. Let me know your location . . . '

Location . . . location . . . location . . . came the soft echoing reply, a sly refrain that sounded strangely like someone else's voice.

The lights had dimmed permanently and Jenna felt the cold tangible presence of fear, like a clutching hand inside her body, squeezing her heart dry. Why hadn't he answered? There was something wrong. She knew without any doubt that something was wrong . . .

'Gan, are you all right?' she tried one last time, and when there was no response knew that it was now up to her. She was alone, no one to help her, and she had to go down there and find out what had happened.

Moving swiftly to a wall locker, Jenna took a gunbelt from the rack and after making sure the power unit was fully charged strapped it on. Its comforting bulk reassured her and she set off along the corridor, trying to convince herself that Gan was really all right, there was nothing to worry about . . . but by the time she had reached the lower hold Jenna's resolve had crumbled because she knew that if humanly possible he would have responded to her urgent pleas.

The door to the lower stern hold was closed. Spinning the locking wheel, she cautiously opened the door and stepped through, her eyes probing the areas of deep shadow.

'Gan . . . ?' she called, her voice strained and tremulous, sounding lost in the vast dark chamber.

All was silent and still. Bracing herself, Jenna began to move slowly forward, keeping close to the bulkhead wall. Every few paces she glanced nervously over her shoulder to reassure herself that the door remained open, knowing it was her only point of escape. Directing her gaze towards the projectile, she didn't see the untidy coil of cables and wires at her feet, and almost fell as she became entangled in them.

That was curious. Jenna frowned as she bent to examine the cable, tracing it with her eyes from where it came out of a small open panel on the projectile and extended across the metalled floor to the link unit on the bulkhead wall. Some- one had made a rough and obviously hasty connection: the front of the link unit had been ripped off and the bare wires joined to the main power source. She could hear a faint crackle as the current coursed through the makeshift arrangement, sparking dangerously. That would explain the drain on the energy supply: someone had tapped the main circuit, drawing off a heavy load.

Could it have been Gan? Jenna wondered, baffled. And if so, why?

Shaking her head perplexedly, she approached the pro- jectile, her attention caught by the pool of water below the hatch. Footprints led away from it, fading after a few paces. Tentatively she raised herself up, peering into the gloomy interior, and again called Gan's name. Then as her eyes grew accustomed to the dim light she registered something that made her heartbeats thud violently in her chest and stifled the breath in her throat.

Both containers were empty.

She had hardly had time to realise the implication of this discovery when there was a loud hollow clang and Jenna whipped round in the hatchway entrance – the door to the hold had been slammed shut!

Scrambling down, she drew the handgun from its holster, making sure that the wire coiling from the butt was firmly connected to the power unit in the belt, and inching her way forward crossed to the bulkhead and flattened her back against it. With the handgun at the ready, she sidled towards the door, her eyes aching with the strain of peering into the shadows, and from above a figure dropped down silently behind her and two powerful hands grasped her round the throat, strangling her.

Jenna lashed out wildly, meeting only empty air, and then with a supreme effort twisted out of his grip and staggered backwards. The man snarled in silent rage and came at her again, his hands reaching out. Jenna fired. A ragged blue light leapt from the muzzle and the fierce impact of the discharge sent him hurtling back against the bulkhead, half of his face gone and his chest in ruins. He slid down in a bloody heap, the life snuffed out of him like a dead candle flame.

Sobbing with relief, Jenna sank to her knees, feeling the cold sweat of fear and exhaustion on her forehead. After a few moments she rose wearily to her feet and was startled by the sound of a low moan. It seemed to be coming from the projectile.

Her hand shaking, Jenna gripped the sidearm and forced herself to step towards the noise; as she did so the same indistinct sound was repeated. Curling her finger round the trigger button in readiness, she was still unprepared as a large broad figure lurched through the gap and almost fell on top of her, collapsing with a stifled groan on to the metalled floor. It was Gan, badly hurt and only just conscious.

Jenna knelt swiftly, holstering the handgun, and cradled his head in her arms. She wiped a smear of blood from his cheek, gazing down at him.

'Easy now,' she murmured gently. 'What happened?'

Gan's lips barely moved. 'Stop them, Jenna.' His eyes were glazed, staring dully past her head. 'You must stop them ...'

'One of them is dead,' she told him rapidly.

Gan tried to focus but he was sliding back into unconsciousness. 'The other one,' she heard him mumble. 'Find him . . . they'll try to take over the ship. Stop them, Jenna . . .'

His eyes closed and his head lolled against her arm.

Jenna lowered him gently to the floor and looked towards the closed door. The blood seemed to roar in her ears. Standing up, she continued to gaze at the bulkhead door, terrified by the immensity of the task which faced her.

Cally dodged nimbly across the narrow space and flattened herself against the wall of a small concrete bunker. She looked to left and right and then nodded sharply, Blake and the others joining her in the protective lee of the building. Above and all around them the towers and masts and dish-shaped radar antenna of the communications complex loomed like spidery metal giants seen through a hazy red mist. They covered a vast area, beaming signals to every part of the galaxy, the nerve-centre of the Federation's electronic web.

Stay under cover until you get my signal, Cally telepathed, preparing to move. Then with an even lithe stride darted on to the next building. Looking back, her eyes fixed unblinkingly on them, her voice echoed in their minds.

It's all right. Come on.

In this piecemeal fashion they slowly progressed deeper into the heart of the complex. At one point they nearly ran headlong into a small Federal patrol and had to dive for cover, holding their breath until the tramp of feet faded away in the distance. Cally seemed to know her way about, and led them unerringly to a long low concrete structure with a bright red diamond painted on the side. Blake guessed that it was a warning symbol of some description.

'What's in here?' he asked her, looking in vain along the featureless walls for any sign of a window.

'Neutron generators,' Cally informed him. 'If we could damage the limiter controls we'd set up a chain reaction that would blow this whole station right off the planet.'

Blake eyed the solid metal door doubtfully. 'We'd need to blast our way in. The explosion would alert the guards before we could do anything.'

'What do you mean?' This in an affronted tone of voice from Vila, who had sidled between them for a closer look. 'Explosives?' He shook his head disgustedly. 'You want the door open – just ask me. Look, I'm a thief, that's my business, opening locked doors.'

'Then go ahead,' Blake invited. 'Open it.'

Vila grinned at him and set to work with a small, multi-pronged metal object. He hummed to himself, happy to be using his skills, and in a matter of seconds there was a click and the door swung open.

'Fantastic,' Blake murmured in genuine appreciation.

'I wouldn't offer to do it if I wasn't good at it,' Vila smirked modestly.

'Watch out!' Avon hissed, and they turned to see a patrol heading towards them. In the same instant they were spotted and there was a good deal of shouting as the guards broke into a run.

'Everybody inside!' Blake snapped, pushing Cally ahead of him, and they all scrambled into a low concrete chamber which contained an array of complex instrumentation. Grabbing whatever was to hand, they had managed to barricade the door just as the guards arrived outside and began pounding on the door with almost inhuman ferocity. The moaning wail of a siren sounded in the distance, to be joined by another, and yet another.

'We won't be able to keep them out for long,' Blake said grimly, raising his voice above the crashing and the shriek of the sirens. 'Avon, this is your area. You know how to accelerate the neutronic discharge.'

Avon was already at the main control panel, examining the dials and gauges. 'Give me a couple of minutes.'

Blake glanced towards the quaking door and then checked his chronometer.

'I'd say that's about all you've got.'

Jenna advanced slowly along the corridor, her finger on the trigger button, cautiously checking each room that she passed. He was somewhere at large in the huge ship, that much was certain, but it was virtually asking the impossible for one person to find him.

Entering the teleport section, she looked fearfully around her, searching behind every piece of equipment that might possibly conceal someone. Satisfied that he wasn't there, she moved to the far door leading to the Flight Deck and operated the control. The door slid open and the man was standing immediately behind it. He seemed huge, framed in the doorway, his eyes fixed upon her with a madman's stare. Even before she had time to scream he made a swift lunging movement, caught hold of the hand holding the gun and twisted it savagely.

Pulling away from him, Jenna tried desperately to break his grip. In the struggle the gun was torn loose from the coiled wire and went spinning across the room.

Jenna scrambled after it frantically. She got her fingers to it and the man came after her and tossed her bodily aside, like a puppet, and she hit the wall, dazed and shaken.

Now he had the gun. A faint frown passed across his heavy, coarse features as, not familiar with the design, he hefted it experimentally and then raised and aimed it. There was no emotion in his face. Pointing it straight at her he pressed the trigger button and Jenna cowered in fearful anticipation.

Her body stiffened involuntarily – but nothing happened.

There was a click from the weapon, and another click as he tried again. Then, flinging it aside, he drew a long knife

197

from a sheath strapped under his arm. Advancing slowly towards Jenna, he raised the knife above his head, and was about to plunge it down upon her defenceless head when the corridor door slid open to reveal Gan. He leaned in the doorway, his face a white mask, his heavy-lidded eyes struggling to remain open.

With an immense effort he raised his gun, the muzzle wavering as he tried to take aim, and then swayed drunkenly, the breath rasping in his throat.

The man could see that Gan was all in. Any moment he might fall. The man had gone very still, his blank mad stare on Gan's face. Very slowly he turned and took a tentative step towards him, then another, calculating the distance between them, preparing for the right moment to spring forward.

Jenna's gun was on the far side of the room. She started to crawl towards it, and as she did so the man moved a pace nearer Gan, to almost within striking distance. Gan was running with sweat. He was pointing the gun at the man's stomach but he couldn't press the trigger. Every nerve was screaming at him to fire but the limiter implanted in his brain had locked his muscles solid.

Still wary, the man took another step forward, and suddenly went for the gun, sweeping it out of Gan's numbed fingers. Jenna made a despairing grab for her own weapon and fumbled to connect the coiled wire to the butt. Her hands were shaking, wasting precious seconds as the man brought his knife up, ready to stab, his lips parted in an insane smile, and Jenna fired.

The knife spun in the air, released from the man's lifeless fingers as the searing blast rammed him against the wall, ripping a hole the size of a fist in his lower back. He slithered down and lay still, seeping and gurgling.

Gan tried to move forward but then he too fell, sprawling unconscious in the centre of the room. Sobbing with relief,

198

Jenna staggered across to him, her voice hoarse and broken, repeating over and over again:

'It's all right now . . . it's over . . . it's over . . . it's over . . .

There were large dents in the metal door and it looked as if at any moment the sustained battering would knock it clean off its hinges. While Vila kept the door covered with his side-arm, Cally helped Blake wedge a steel cabinet in position. Avon had removed a panel from one of the consoles and was probing into the maze of electronic circuitry, trying to trace the automatic fail-safe device.

'We can't hold them much longer,' Blake warned him, afraid to take his eyes off the bulging door.

'I'm nearly there . . . ' Avon muttered, his face creased in anguished concentration.

Vila touched Blake's shoulder and pointed to a gauge on which the pointer was slowly creeping into the red.

'It's running up into the danger level.'

Avon glanced up at the gauge and spoke tersely over his shoulder. 'I still have to disconnect the automatic shut-offs. If I don't, the safety circuits will close down the reactors.'

Blake took a teleport bracelet from his pocket and handed it to Cally. She examined it curiously.

'Put this on.'

'What is it?'

'Our escape route. Put it on!' he ordered sternly when she hesitated.

There was a tremendous crash from the door and the steel cabinet nearly heeled over. Blake and Cally braced themselves against it.

'Make it fast,' Blake called over his shoulder, gritting his teeth as another crash reverberated through the concrete room.

*

Jenna knelt at Gan's side, calmer now that the danger had passed. Relief was like a soothing balm. She was brought back to herself as the lights dimmed, and leaning close to his ear she spoke clearly and precisely so that he would understand.

'Gan. I have to leave you. They had linked up their ship to our primary power system. We're getting a heavy energy loss. I have to disconnect. Will you be all right?'

Gan nodded weakly. Jenna rose to her feet, feeling stronger and more in control now that she had nothing to fear. Turning resolutely to the door she stepped into the corridor and set off briskly for the lower hold. On the Flight Deck, the black auto-nav box had yielded up its secrets to the computer. The sequence of lights on the panel flashed their varied permutations and Zen's soft emotionless voice intoned to the silent empty room:

'Decoding on the projectile's auto-log is now complete. Logic circuits have analysed the principal information. The occupants have been identified as an assassination squad. Their mission is to destroy political leaders on the planet Velgan. They have been indoctrinated to the point of fanaticism and conditioned to allow nothing to keep them from accomplishing their mission. The squad consists of four – note FOUR – operatives, the commander's cryo support system being located in the rear of the projectile ...'

Jenna entered the lower hold and straight away went across to the projectile and examined the cable connection in the small open panel. This shouldn't take long, she reckoned, though it might be wise to disconnect the link unit first – the bare wires were a definite fire hazard.

Moving quickly to a workbench, she began to sort through some tools, turning her back on the now harmless projectile. Inside the projectile, the locking wheel on the door at the rear of the compartment started to turn, slowly and silently, operated from the other side.

200

Unsuspecting, Jenna selected the tools she required and moved to the link unit with its torn-off panel in the bulkhead. Her hands still shook a little, though now she was much calmer, knowing the danger had passed, and she set to work with a light heart to repair the damage.

The metal door was caving in, no longer able to resist the fierce onslaught from the Federal guards. Only seconds remained.

Avon located the vital connection, severed the wires, and let out a triumphant yell. 'That's it! It'll go now, there's nothing can stop it!'

Watching the needle in the gauge swing across the red scale, Blake raised the bracelet to his lips and snapped an urgent command.

'We're ready . . . bring us up!'

Lying on the floor of the teleport section, Gan heard Blake's voice issuing from the speaker. Mustering all his strength, he began to crawl painfully towards the control panel.

'Jenna . . . Gan . . . operate the controls! Now! You hear me! Now!'

Exhausted by his efforts, Gan slumped down, feeling the strength ebb away from him.

In the neutron chamber, the first low rumblings of the gathering explosion were beginning to shake the fabric of the building. The needle was right over to the limit on the red scale.

'It's going!' Avon screamed hoarsely. 'It's going up!'

'Teleport!' Blake shouted into the communicator. 'Now!'

Gan reached the control panel and through a swirling mist of pain and utter exhaustion raised himself up, his hand seeking the vital control. The rows of buttons, dials and gauges swam crazily before his eyes, his hand hovering as he tried to focus.

Blake and the others fell back as an intense white light began to fill the chamber. Dust showered all around as the rumbling built up to a thunderous peak – and mingled with the sound an horrendous ripping of metal as the door was wrenched off its hinges and the guards started to clamber in.

With a final supreme effort, Gan pressed the teleport control, then slid semi-conscious to the floor.

Blake, Cally, Vila and Avon began to dematerialise in the very same instant that the neutron explosion erupted. The guards swarmed into the chamber and in the last split-second of existence saw the four figures vanish as everything was transformed into blinding white light and heat.

The neutron chain reaction flowered like a poppy expanding in water and obliterated them from the face of the planet.

Blake and the others materialised in the teleport section. Taking in the situation at a glance, Blake ran across and stopped by Gan's inert body.

'Where's Jenna?'

Gan's lips moved feebly, hardly able to form the words. 'In the hold . . .'

'Take care of him,' Blake rapped at the others, and even as he spoke was bounding for the door.

He was a shadow – huge, silent, menacing. Crouched by the open hatch, his hooded maniac's eyes watched the girl's slim back as it bent assiduously to the task of restoring the power loss to the *Liberator*'s primary energy source. Jenna was totally absorbed in her work, oblivious to his presence, but even so he moved with the stealth and cold deadly purpose of the trained assassin.

There was a single word imprinted on the cells of his brain: a compulsive and irreversible command. The word was *kill*.

And for such a big man he was incredibly light on his feet, each movement co-ordinated and controlled with the hypnotic grace of a snake preparing to strike. Still keeping his eyes fixed on her, his hand crept towards the sheath strapped beneath his arm and slowly withdrew the long gleaming blade.

He moved inexorably towards her, raising the knife, selecting the precise point on the nape of her neck where a swift bloody slash would sever her central nervous system. He was trained not to make mistakes, and with a target as easy and inviting as this there wouldn't be any.

He stood close behind her, near enough to hear her light shallow breathing, the knife gripped firmly in his right hand. The powerful muscles in his arm and shoulder contracted, preparing to deliver the death blow. A hollow clang boomed out as the bulkhead door was kicked savagely open and Blake burst into the hold. His warning yell alerted Jenna as the knife plunged downwards and she twisted aside, the blade missing her by inches.

Bracing himself, both hands gripping the gun at arm's length, Blake let loose a dazzling ribbon of ragged blue fire which hit the assassin full in the chest and hurled him backwards against the bulkhead. His flailing arm touched the bare cable and he was engulfed in a crackling shower of sparks as the ship's tremendous voltage surged through his body. In seconds nothing remained but a charred hulk, a cinder in the shape of a man.

Jenna stared horrified, seeing the long shining knife still clamped in the blackened fingers, and turned away, her head buried in her shaking hands.

Everyone was silent, watching the pattern of neutron explosions on the large screen; they appeared like tiny glow-worms brightening and fading on the dark side of the planet.

They were all standing, except Gan, who lay on one of the deeply padded control chairs, his left arm in a sling, looking like a volunteer from first-aid practice. But his rugged face still wore a weary yet indefatigable grin.

Blake turned from the screen and glanced at Cally. 'It will take them a long time to build up their communications network again,' he observed with grim satisfaction.

Cally's eyes held his for a fleeting moment, and in his mind Blake heard her voice murmur gratefully:

Thank you.

Blake smiled his acknowledgement. 'You can't go back to Saurian Major,' he told her. 'Is there somewhere we can take you?'

Cally shrugged and looked away. 'I've nowhere to go.'

'Then stay with us,' Blake offered.

'Can I?' Her voice was unsure and eager at the same time.

'Glad to have you,' Blake said warmly. 'With you we've got a full crew. We're up to seven.'

Vila nodded happily and then his face suddenly changed. 'Seven?' he queried, making a quick count. 'Six.'

'And Zen makes seven,' Blake grinned. He leaned across to the receptor panel. 'Stand by for course and speed.'

The *Liberator* was up to strength with a full crew.

Blake's Seven.

The massive ship began to move away from Saurian Major, accelerating as she forged deeper into space, heading for distant star systems and adventures as yet unknown.

NOW OVER 5 MILLION COPIES WORLDWIDE!

STAR WARS

George Lucas

THE INTERNATIONALLY BEST-SELLING SPACE ADVENTURE EPIC

With 16 pages of full colour stills from the film!

'MARVELLOUS SPACE OPERA STUFF ... IF THE FILM IS AS MUCH FUN, I CAN HARDLY WAIT TO SEE IT'
Daily Mirror

Farm chores sure could be dull, and Luke Sykwalker was bored beyond belief. He yearned for adventures out among the stars – adventures that would take him beyond the furthest galaxies to distant and alien worlds.

But Luke got more than he bargained for when he intercepted a cryptic message from a beautiful princess held captive by a dark and powerful warlord. Luke didn't know who she was, but he knew he had to save her – and soon, because time was running out.

Armed only with courage and with the light sabre that had been his father's, Luke was catapulted into the middle of the most savage space-war ever ... and he was headed straight for a desperate encounter on the enemy battle station known as the Death Star!

0 7221 5669 3   SCIENCE FICTION/FILM TIE IN   95p

THE DANCER FROM ATLANTIS
Poul Anderson

Duncan Reid was snatched out of the twentieth
century from a cruise liner in the mid-Pacific. . . .
Oleg Vladimirovitch came from Novgorod in
mediaeval Russia. . . .
Uldin was a Hun barbarian who lived by cunning and
the axe. . . . Erissa had been a sacred priestess in a
lost continent. . . . And a mistake in a time-experiment
by a race from the far future had thrown these four
unlikely comrades together, pulling them through a
warp in the fabric of space and time to a world
which was ancient history. The strange alliance that
Duncan and his companions formed in that unfamiliar
world was to take on a significance that none of
them could have foreseen. For not only their own
future, but the very future of the world they had
found was at stake. . . .

WAR OF THE WING MEN
THREE HEARTS AND THREE LIONS
THE BROKEN SWORD

0 7221 1163 0   SCIENCE FICTION   75p

CLASSIC SF SHORT STORIES –
'THE BEST OF' SERIES

Isaac Asimov (1939-1952)   65p

Isaac Asimov (1954-1972)   65p

John W. Campbell   75p

Arthur C. Clarke (1937-1955)   65p

Arthur C. Clarke (1956-1972)   75p

Robert A. Heinlein (1939-1942)   65p

Robert A. Heinlein (1947-1959)   65p

Frank Herbert (1952-1964)   75p

Frank Herbert (1965-1970)   75p

Fritz Leiber   60p

Clifford D. Simak   60p

A. E. Van Vogt   60p

John Wyndham (1932-1949)   65p

John Wyndham (1951-1960)   65p

All Sphere Books are available at your bookshop or newsagent, or can be ordered from the following address: Sphere Books, Cash Sales Department, P.O. Box 11, Falmouth, Cornwall.

Please send cheque or postal order (no currency), and allow 19p for postage and packing for the first book plus 9p per copy for each additional book ordered up to a maximum charge of 73p in U.K.

Customers in Eire and B.F.P.O. please allow 19p for postage and packing for the first book plus 9p per copy for the next 6 books, thereafter 3p per book.

Overseas customers please allow 20p for postage and packing for the first book and 10p per copy for each additional book.